HOW NOT TO KILL DRAGONS

A JOURNAL BY SIR KRISTOFF BROLAWSKIIVEN

R. JOY

This book is dedicated to my brother in law Chris!
You helped brainstorm this book into being as we worked on the farm, and
are the namesake for Sir Kristoff. Thanks for all the inspiration!

FOREWORD

Join my Monthly Fantasy Periodical to get a FREE short story! In my periodical you'll get to have some fantasy fun with me, solve riddles, get exclusive sneak peaks at my upcoming books, and even help me with titles and character names.

You can sign up through my website https://rjoyfantasy.wixsite.com/my-site-1 and claim your free short story!

CONTENTS

Map of Kelasinar .1   VI

Map of Kelasinar .2   VII

1. Kelasinar   1

2. Dalnar   26

3. Arrovad   43

Map of Taruvek .1   60

Map of Taruek .2   61

4. Taruvek   62

Afterword   80

Also By   81

Acknowledgments   82

About Author   84

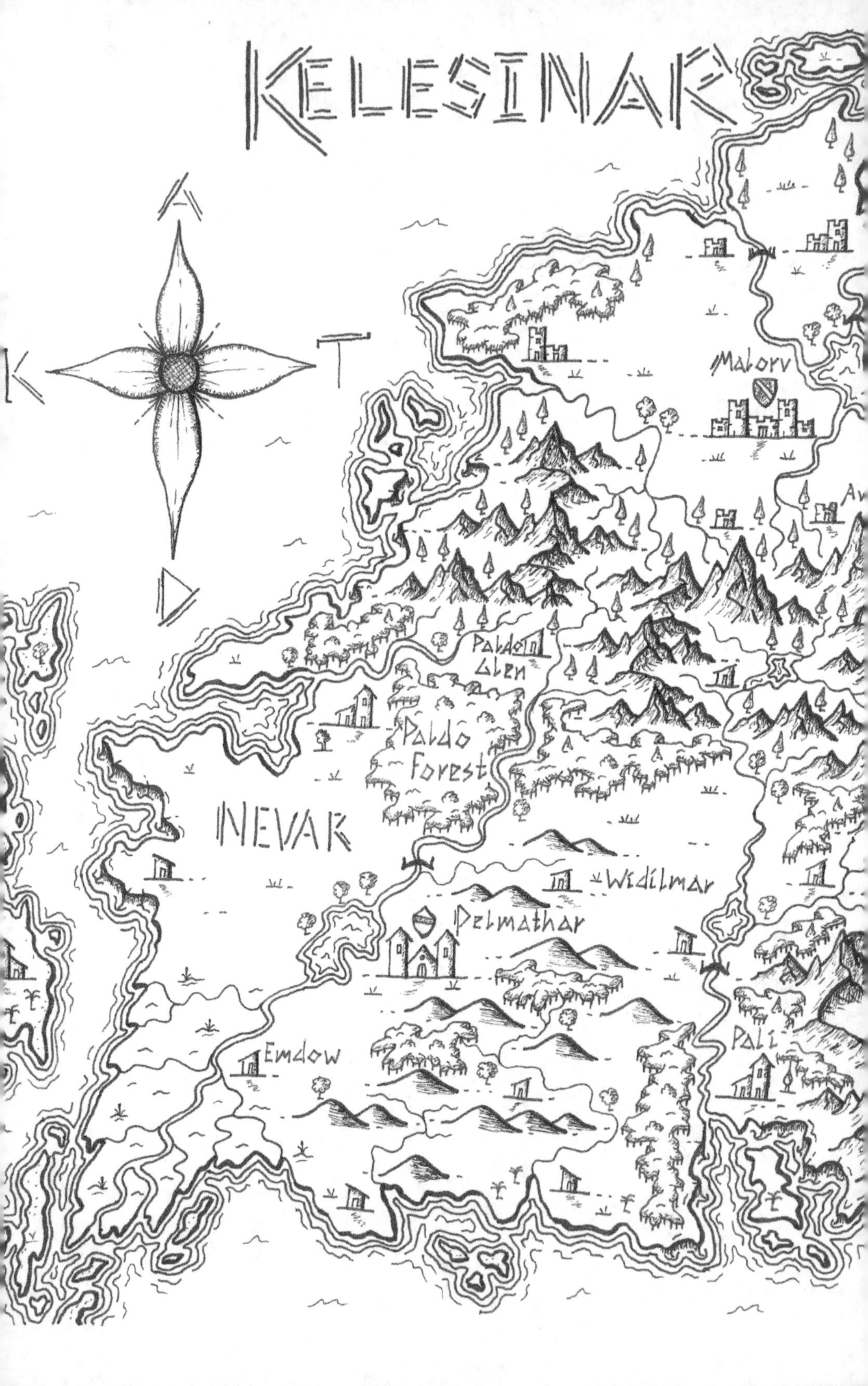

KELESINAK
K
T
Malorv
Paldon Glen
Paldo Forest
NEVAR
Widilmar
Pelmathar
Pali
Emdow

BILDAR
Breknal
Asberglen
Felmi
Viscon
KASGAR
3-22

Kelasinar

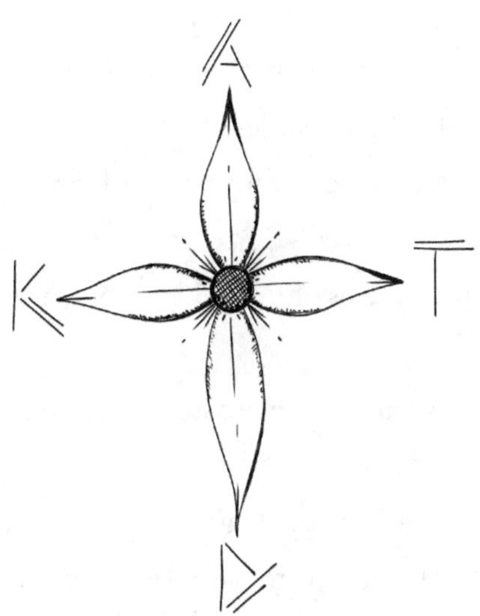

Tertius, the 33rd day of Ver, 2,633ALD

First entry, by Sir Kristoff of Brolawskiiven Manor.

In this journal I shall record my adventures, victories, and what I learn as I travel the world hunting down dragons to mount their heads on my trophy wall. I want our story to be published and read around the world, and I hope to be remembered as a Legend one day.

Taruvek, where I hail from, no longer has any dragons due to two major disasters that occurred centuries ago that nearly wiped out all life on Taruvek. The first was the Lunar Disintegration which affected every continent in one way or another (but Taruvek especially), and the second was the Days of Darkness, a great volcanic eruption that once again nearly wiped out the continent. So we are beginning our journey on Kelasinar, the land with the largest population of dragons in the world. The people here widely accept dragons into their society as if they're intelligent beasts. To me that is just nonsense; if a creature can't talk it isn't intelligent, and since dragons can't talk well then it's obvious they aren't smart.

Kelasinar has a similar climate to ours, with both cold and hot seasons, but not to the extremes of Arrovad or Dalnar.

The dragons we will be hunting here are the Galewing, the Firetalon, the Marshback, and lastly the Timebender.

Joining me on this quest are ten of my friends from Taruvek, each wanting to add a dragon head to their wall. Since I came up with this quest I will be leading it, and at eighteen cycles old, I feel I am mature enough to be a good leader.

I am unsure what calendar the other continents use, so for those who may read this and are unfamiliar with the Taruveken one, it goes like this: there are four months in each five hundred day sun cycle, each corresponding with a season, and each is one hundred and twenty-five days long. The first is Ver, the month of new growth and life; then Aestas, the hottest month; Cado (my birth month), the month of harvest; and Hiems, the coldest month. Our weeks are five days long, and the first day of the week is Primus, then Secundus, Tertius, Quartus, and Quintus. The directional words they use around the world may be different as well, but on Taruvek we use these for the corresponding points of our compass: Arro where the frosts fall first, Tar where the sun rises, Daln where summer lasts the longest, and Kel where the sun sets.

Anyway, the first dragon we are hunting is the Galewing. It lives on the plains of Bildar, one of the three countries of Kelasinar. Aestas is when their breeding season begins, so right now they are likely getting into prime physique to attract their mates. I expect we'll find them hunting the herds of longhorn bison that graze the plains.

Quintus, 35th day of Ver.

Today we stopped in an idyllic town called Asberglen, midway between the Tar coast where we made landfall, and the Silken Plains. Most of the people here seem healthy and happy; Bildar must be a thriving country for a town so far from the capital to be doing so well. Apparently Bildar is what they call a matriarchy with an oligarchical government, so most of the mayors and town leaders are women. Back on Taruvek there were many women in power, but also many men.

When we went to the market to buy some food and other supplies, John, one of my companions, bought each of his six children a little trinket, and a wooden necklace for his wife, since wood is so rare on our continent. I asked him if he was sure he wanted to carry those the whole trip, and he said he would pay to have an extra pack animal if he must, so that he could bring his family gifts from each continent.

As I watched John buy his things from the shopkeeper, I realized once again just how different we look from the people here. John's skin is sand colored compared to the woman's deep golden brown tones, his hair a dark brown in stark contrast to her soft golden-blonde waves, and her vibrant green eyes look very different next to his steel gray, almond-shaped ones. Overall the people here have a very warm look to them, like a sunset through leaves that are just beginning to change color in Cado.

Secundus, 37th day of Ver.

I couldn't believe my eyes when we reached the Silken Plains of Bildar!

As soon as I walked amongst the waist-high jade grass covering this vast flat plain, I understood why they called it that. The blades run through your fingers like the smoothest of fabrics, and as the ever-present wind blows through the grass, it makes a gentle whispering sound as if there are voices taunting us, and it carries with it the delicate sweet scent of honey. The only thing to be seen for miles, aside from the grass, is a random scrubby tree here and there. It reminds me of home, and I briefly felt a bit homesick looking at it.

The animals here are abundant, though. We've seen herds of longhorn bison, flocks of Titanis birds, a few massive rare white lions which live solitary lives, and even a pride of their smaller cousin the black lion. White-striped gray wolves run in packs of up to twenty strong here, and there is an animal they hunt known as the mammoth wildebeest that roams in huge herds across the land, leaving the grass eaten short in their wake.

My friend Mark, the true trophy hunter, wants to hunt down a lion of each color and bring their heads home with him, but this idea was vetoed by Sir Tobias and I, the oldest member in our company, as we need to stay focused on our quest.

Tobias has carefully planned out which order we should hunt the dragons based on their locations, breeding seasons, and nesting seasons. I am thankful he is so knowledgeable in preparing for such things from his years serving as a knight, as that is not my area of expertise.

As we travel, Tom, the bard, sings us ballads. So though we haven't spotted a Galewing yet, morale remains high among the men.

Quintus, 40th day of Ver.

We saw our first Galewing today!

It dove out of the wispy clouds and took down a longhorn bison about a mile away. Its long, slender body was covered in small overlapping scales the color of moonstones, with soft snow-white feathers on the edges of its translucent wings and down its spine. The span of its shimmering wings must have been nearly one hundred feet!

The sheer power and grace of this creature was astounding. As it dove from the clouds towards its prey like a giant falcon, the sun glinted off its scales and wings and momentarily blinded me. In seconds, it had the bison pinned beneath its claws, the neck broken. I watched it in mesmerization as it leapt back up into the sky again, beating its gigantic wings to lift its heavy prey from the ground.

Seeing it honestly left me breathless. It will be something I remember for the rest of my days: the moment I first saw a living, breathing dragon.

Secundus, 42nd day of Ver.

The men have placed bets on who will kill the first dragon. Most are in Mark's favor since he has the most trophies of any of us already, but several of us have placed our bets on Ed, since he's the best tracker. Regardless of who gets the first kill, we are bound and determined that we will hunt down enough dragons for each of us to have our own head and whatever else we want.

Tertius, 43rd day of Ver.

A great roar startled us from our sleep last night!

It was like rushing wind combined with the deep groaning a forest makes under the strength of a gale just before trees start to snap.

We all leapt from our bedrolls with our harpoon guns drawn, but when we searched the area the dragon was not there, so we set a watch for the night.

Our plan for killing this dragon is to capture a living longhorn bison, if we can, and then tie it up and leave it out to attract a Galewing. We will sell the horses in the next village, attach grass to our cloaks, and lie in wait for a dragon to come. I'm confident our plan will work, as this is a tactic Mark has used to lure predators many times back on Taruvek.

Before we retire each night Tom entertains us with tales and songs from home, many of them revolving around the Legends of the Shadow Wars. Some of the tales he tells I have not heard before, but I have not traveled Taruvek as extensively as he has. It was the first Legend, Captain Dwyn, who figured out how to build ships big enough to sail across the ocean and discovered these continents. I hope I am remembered for my great deeds on this quest like her. Though it seems the quickest way to become a Legend is to wage war against the gods of Shadow like she and the others did...

Quartus, 44th day of Ver.

An unnatural wind buffets us from every angle as we ride.

Because of this, my poor lips taste like iron when I lick them and my hands are cracked and bleeding where they have dried out.

By evening we reached a small village called Breknal, which is constructed entirely from wood. It is very strange to see buildings built out of wood, since on Taruvek wood is rare because of the Lunar Disintegration and the Days of Darkness, the two disasters that wiped out the dragons and most other life. A type of ironwood is our currency which we call Shard Rings. Meanwhile, metal is common back home because so much was unearthed when the asteroid from the Lunar Disintegration struck our continent, hence we build our homes from it. Here on Kelasinar as a whole it is the opposite. They have many forest regions with more varieties of trees in each one than in all of Taruvek, but they don't have as much metal, so that is their currency in the form of discs.

Fortunately as we went through the village towards the tavern, a healer named Alyanna saw the state we were in with our bleeding lips and hands, and she took pity on us foreigners. She sold us soft beeswax at a discount to help our skin stay moist in the dry air here. It has worked like a charm from the gods of Light themselves. She then proceeded to invite us to her home for a meal of fried grouse, mashed turnips, and pickled radish salad. As we consumed the surprisingly delicious food, she told us tales of her country and of the dragons here, some of which I'm sure were exaggerated. She asked us all about Taruvek. She was quite shocked that the dragons were all wiped out, and when she heard that the volcano eruption that caused the twelve Days of Darkness was caused by the dragons and riders themselves, she was even more amazed.

Unfortunately, we couldn't get much useful information on the dragon's weaknesses from her without revealing our purpose here. Before we left, Frank had her write down the recipes for each of the foods she served us, and she did so with a smile. Oddly Frank came on this quest because he wants to find out what dragon meat tastes like, the thought of which is disgusting to me, but I'm happy he came because none of the others can cook nearly as well as he can.

After leaving her home we stopped at the market to stock up on supplies again; Frank bought some more food for the journey, and then we sold our horses to the local stable.

As we expected, we have no way of restocking our harpoon gun bolts here because they use weapons they call "longbows" for long-ranged attacks. Thankfully we brought extra ones with us just in case they didn't have them.

Quintus, 45th day of Ver.
After leaving Breknal and traveling for a day on foot, we had some luck and caught an injured longhorn bison!

Our trap is set, our cloaks covered in long blades of silk grass, and now we lie in wait for our prey. As we lay there I overheard Joe, the youngest member of our company, telling Tom next to him about a girl he had met back home before he left. It seems he has a sweetheart he didn't tell us about. I'm sure she'll be impressed when he comes home from this quest with the head of a dragon to mount on his wall.

Quintus, 45th day of Ver. Later in the day...

No signs of the dragon.

Strangely enough, even the wind has gone still. The bison has the right idea and is taking a nap now. I feel a bit bad for the poor creature and its fate.

Joe can't seem to stop talking as we wait. His excitement about the hunt rivals that of even Charles, who's the biggest optimist I know. After hours of it, I'm starting to get a bit annoyed.

Primus, 46th day of Ver.

Still, we wait.

We've split ourselves into two groups, and while one goes over a hill to eat, relieve themselves, and take a quick nap, the other group stays to keep watch. After each group took their turn to eat we regrouped to sit and watch together. I think Ed fell asleep a bit ago, even though he's supposed to be the best tracker in the group.

Secundus, 47th day of Ver.

The Galewing found us, and young Joe is dead.

Dawn was just lighting the sky through a thick fog bank and we were setting up camp, exhausted after having waited all day on Quintus and Primus, and all night last night for it to appear. That's when a strong wind whipped away the mists and the Galewing appeared from straight above us, dropping down almost on top of us.

We scrambled to draw our harpoon guns, but before we could, it blasted most of us with a gust of wind so strong it knocked us down. When Joe and Tom charged it from the other side, it whipped its tail at them, knocking Tom down. Then I saw its blue topaz eyes look straight at Joe, who had leapt over its tail, before it blasted him about twenty feet back with a burst of powerful air magic. He slammed into one of the only trees on this empty plain and fell to the ground, dead.

As we bellowed our fury and grief to the wind, we tried to pick ourselves up to fight, the dragon leapt into the air while overpowering us with another strong wind, knocking us all back to the ground...again.

The feeling of its magic lingered in the air as the wind resumed its normal gentle whispering.

When our healer, Steffan, checked Tom, he wasn't badly hurt, but was bruised where the dragon's tail struck him across the belly and chest, and still a bit breathless from having the air knocked out of him.

We gathered Joe's body, wrapped him in his cloak, and then tied him to a travois we built from the tree that killed him, before leaving the site of his untimely death.

I caught myself looking at the group as we walked, expecting to see Joe chatting with one of the men, but instead he's covered up and lying on the travois. He was too young to die like this, and I'm saddened that his sweetheart back home will never see him again. I must not show my weakness in front of the others though, so I shall mourn for him later in private.

The small village of Breknal is the closest, so we are returning there to bury his body. We'll decide what we should do after that.

Tertius, 48th day of Ver.
We buried Joe just outside of Breknal.

Afterwards, we planted a seed of the kunu nut tree from our home continent Taruvek above him and said a prayer to the Seven gods of Light, as is our tradition back home. The local priests were generous enough to agree to continue to care for the tree and honor our friend with a prayer every year on this day.

I feel like I failed Joe as a friend and the leader of this company. I pray the gods give him a place in their kingdom on the sun from where he can watch us. That way he can see us finish this quest in his honor.

After the burial, we stayed at the inn for a day while we discussed what to do next. Steffan and Rick, the ex-spy, were arguing that we should stay and hunt the Galewing down to avenge Joe, while Ed and John are very much against the idea. I hadn't yet made up my mind on what we should do, so I silently listened to both sides of the argument.

At one point Steffan yelled at them, saying, "Are you just going to let that Galewing win, then? It killed our friend! The least we can do to avenge him is kill the beast in return!"

In his usual calm, deep voice, Tobias interrupted the argument, saying, "We cannot avenge him because we will never find that same Galewing again on this huge open plain. Instead we should honor his memory by continuing the quest as Joe would want to do himself if he were with us. Besides, we need to reach the Firetalon dragon's territory and kill one soon. As it stands, many of them will have a mate already which makes hunting them harder and more dangerous for us. Not to mention that the closer we get to when they start laying in Aestas the more their hormones will be raging and the more aggressive they will be."

I stood up then, having made up my mind, and said, "Sir Tobias is right. There's no sense hunting down a dragon we will never be able to find again on this vast plain. No, if we wish to succeed in killing the rest of the dragons on our list, we must continue as planned."

Steffan finally calmed down after a bit more convincing (mostly by Sir Tobias, the voice of reason). I could tell he and Mark were sore about the subject, but they let it go as we all went to bed, exhausted from our day.

Quartus, 49th day of Ver.

The mood is somber as we ride towards the mountains.

Sir Tobias had served under Joe's father and looked up to him, before he died in the Shadow Wars, so Sir Tobias swore to watch over Joe in his place. This is why Joe's death has hit him especially hard. He rides at the back alone, his hood pulled up over his head even in the warm sunlight. Once in a while when I look back, I think I see his shoulders shaking, as if he might be weeping.

Primus, 51st day of Ver.

We've been on the road for three days now, and by the map we're still three days' ride away from the small town we'll be stopping in next. We are headed for the volcano, Quovig, in the Kasgarian branch of the Great Dividing Mountain chain called the Dragon's Maw. We hope to find the Firetalons there, bathing in the volcano's lava pools as they are said to do.

Firetalons, or Eruptorectums as they're commonly called, are extremely dangerous with their lava breath, fiery talons and spikes, and the extreme heat they can bring to an area just by being there.

Some accounts even say that they got their common name because they are easily startled, and some react like a skunk does when that happens. But I'm not sure I believe this, as it seems too far-fetched for such a huge and dangerous predator.

We'll need to be careful as we travel through the mountains though, because the paths up to the volcano are said to be treacherous.

At midday we stopped to water the horses we bought in Breknal at a stream. While they drank, since Primus is our holy day, we said our prayers to the Lights, and I think we were all saying them with Joe in mind. After that we had a quick meal, which Frank whipped up for us, before getting back on the road.

Quartus, 54th day of Ver.

We are barely a day into the Dragon's Maw and already several of us have fallen and cut ourselves on the jagged rocks we are climbing. Whoever said this was the best path to take must have been blind or insane, because this is no path.

Thank goodness we stopped in the mountain town of Felmi to restock our supplies and sell our horses, because if we hadn't I'm fairly certain they and we would be dead by now.

The heat of the desert sun is scorching our backs, even though it's still Ver and not even Aestas yet, and the sharp black rocks burn and cut us from beneath. It is truly no wonder they call this the Dragon's Maw.

None of us are speaking at the moment due to the bad conditions, our exhaustion, and the recent death. Even Charles, our optimist, seems down, and Tom hasn't told a story or sung a song all day.

Primus, 56th day of Ver.

The heat is even more extreme now that we've reached Quovig, the volcano.

Last night we camped at the base of the volcano, and while Frank was cooking a desert hare that Ed tracked down and shot with his harpoon gun, he forgot to take into account how hot the air is here, and the hare became a bit...I hate to say it, but burnt. In all the years I've eaten Frank's food nothing has been burnt, but this hare was. None of us dared say a word about it though, as Frank very aggressively portioned it onto our plates as if to say, "One word and you'll end up like the hare!" It was hard, but we all managed to swallow it down without emptying our stomachs.

We are now picking our way up the slopes with great care because there are active lava flows coming down it. We have soaked our clothes in what water we could spare and wrapped our hands in wet cloth to protect them from the hot rocks. Sir Tobias and I had to leave our chainmail at the base of the volcano with all of the heavier supplies. I feel naked with only my leather armor to protect me, but even leaving things behind we're still drenched in sweat.

We briefly saw a fire opal-colored Eruptorectum with red sapphire wings fly into a cave near the top of the volcano, but it will take us at least a day to climb up there without killing ourselves in the process.

My plan is to catch it while it's in the cave and block the entrance to trap it. We'll have to kill it quickly with our harpoon guns once we have it trapped, because if we wait too long it will breathe lava at us.

Secundus, 57th day of Ver.

Charles made a grave mistake.

When we finally reached the dragon's cave, he went in first, and as soon as he stepped around the corner he was surprised to see the Eruptorectum's backend literally right in front of him, and he swore loudly, saying, "Great dung piles!" which of course startled the dragon.

Unfortunately for Charles, it seems the accounts about Eruptorectums being like skunks when they're startled was correct. But when an Eruptorectum farts, it's not just regular smelly gas that's released; it's a sulfur-smelling gas which burns your skin and eyes, and it's very deadly when breathed in high concentrations.

He dropped dead with another curse on his lips, and Sir Tobias, who was several feet behind him, stumbled back coughing and grabbing his throat, but thankfully he didn't breathe in as much since he was farther back.

As the Eruptorectum swung around to face us we were all scrambling back, holding our breaths while trying not to fall. A moment later it poked its fire opal head out of the cave, its talons and spikes blazing with blue fire, as it breathed lava down the trail after us, which sent us running and stumbling away.

Most of us made it away even more bloodied, sweating, and gasping for air than before. Tobias especially was struggling for air since he breathed in some of the dragon's fart. John got burned badly on his leg by a splash of dragon lava and was being helped along by Steffan.

We will have to get them both to the nearest village as quickly as possible, and unfortunately Charles' body will have to be left behind.

I am numb after what just happened. Charles was such a good friend, and he always looks for... I mean, looked for the best in every situation. I don't know what we will do without his upbeat presence to keep us going.

Quintus, 60th day of Ver.

We have made camp and I am writing this by the dying fire.

The last three days have been grueling. We barely stopped to rest as we fled the Dragon's Maw because we saw the Eruptorectum flying behind us several times.

Thankfully Steffan is a good enough healer that he stabilized both Tobias and John as we fled. John's leg is very badly burned, and when I pulled Steffan aside to ask about it he said, "He may never walk the same again. The burn went deep into the muscle. At this point I can only do my best to keep it clean and from getting infected."

After that conversation, I knew we would likely be saying goodbye to John at the next town.

Secundus, 62nd day of Ver.

Tomorrow is Sir Tobias' birth month celebration day; he'll be thirty-one cycles old.

On Taruvek everyone born in the same month celebrates their birth on the sixty-third day of that month each year, so it's always a massive celebration with food, drinks, and gifts.

Unfortunately, it won't be a very happy celebration for Tobias since he is currently in the infirmary of a small town called Avoro which we managed to limp to.

Plus, now both Joe and poor Charles are dead, which makes this birth month celebration even worse for him.

We've all taken to calling Charles "poor Charles" because no man should die the way he did. We shall have to tell his family he died fighting a great Firetalon because death by dragon fart is not at all heroic or honorable, let alone believable. We planted a veil tree in his honor just outside of town and said prayers for him since we cannot bury his body.

As expected, John is on his way back to a port town to board a ship sailing for Taruvek. At least he will be reunited with his twelve kids soon. He is also bringing word back to Joe and poor Charles' families about their fate.

I can only hope we do better on our future hunts, as thus far they have gone very badly.

Quintus, 65th day of Ver.

For two days now we've been riding towards the wetlands of Nevar, the third and final country of Kelasinar.

Tom has begun writing a song about our quest, and as we travel the world he will keep adding to it. Maybe one day we will be remembered and sung about as the Legends of the Shadow Wars are. He sings of our sorrow over our fallen friends, but also of our wonder at the new land we are in. It appears he and I are recording this journey in different ways.

Secundus, 67th day of Ver.

The hills we have been traveling through as we head towards the wetlands are beautiful and vast, with an abundance of wildlife and forests between the farms and small towns.

We are currently staying the night in a village called Widilmar, and they have been very welcoming to us. We found out in the tavern that we were not the first Taruvekens that have stayed here. In fact, three Legends from the Shadow Wars stayed here just six years ago. Seems the people here remember them well as one of the Legends helped prevent a tornado from destroying their village, and thus they welcomed us with open arms.

The food here on Kelasinar is very different from what we're used to eating on Taruvek. They love to fry and grill their food here, and they also eat a lot of what they call beef as well as other meats, and lots of beans, potatoes, and corn.

With how the people here in Nevar talk about dragons and the Dragon Riders with such high respect and esteem, I'm not sure they'd agree with our quest. So instead of telling them about it, we just told them we were traveling the world to write about each of the different cultures and the dragons, which is actually partially true, given what I'm writing now.

We should reach the wetlands within a day, and there we will begin our hunt for the Marshback.

The rest of us are nearly recovered from the cuts and burns we received except for the deepest ones, but we should still be up for the fight. Marshbacks aren't as large as Galewings or Eruptorectums, so I'm certain we will kill one.

Quartus, 69th day of Ver.

We are in the wetlands now.

The bugs are very thick here, and many of us are scratching and sweaty already from the high humidity.

There will be one more town for us to stay in before we journey deeper into the swamps to the places the Marshbacks live.

Quintus, 70th day of Ver.

We are deep in the swamps now.

We had to leave our horses in the stilt town called Emdow, as the landscape here is too treacherous for them to traverse.

All of us have slipped into the murky water already. And now we are getting eaten alive by the massive bugs that love this moist, humid place.

I hope we get that dragon soon, or there may not be much of us left to hunt it once the bugs are through with us.

Secundus, 72nd day of Ver.

I hate swamps.

They are wretched places, with nothing good in them. We haven't seen any signs of Marshbacks. Plus, oddly there is an inordinate number of logs floating along with us, though there aren't many trees nor much of a current in these swamps...

Quartus, 74th day of Ver.

It's raining now, which makes the humidity even more unbearable.

The clouds hang low and heavy over us, a mist floats just above the murky water, and our cloaks and packs are completely soaked through. I'm thankful this journal is made out of waterproof hides, not paper like Kelasinarians use, so it has not gotten ruined.

Somehow there are more logs than ever floating along as we trudge through the swamp. Mark threw rocks at them for fun, but even with his good aim he could never seem to hit them. Then a short while later he lost a boot when he got stuck in a deep pit of mud that seemed to just melt beneath his feet, even though we had all just walked over it before him.

Thankfully Ed had a spare pair along, so he borrowed one from him, though it's a bit small for him.

If only Charles was still with us. Somehow I feel like he could make a joke about this whole experience and make us laugh a little.

When we finally do find a Marshback we will need to get the net we bought in Emdow over it quickly to keep it from getting back into the swamps, then we will be able to kill it.

Quintus, 75th day of Ver.

They weren't logs!

We set up camp last night in the rain, and we woke up to Mark yelling as he disappeared completely into some mud that appeared beneath his bedroll. Just then, the rest of us realized we were slowly sinking down as well, and it was chaos for several long minutes as we struggled against the mud swallowing us alive.

That's when I saw them. All those "logs" floating in the swamp had glowing orange eyes that were trained on us as we struggled.

I naturally grabbed my harpoon gun and started firing into the darkness at the logs with eyes, but they all sank beneath the water. The mud stopped sucking us down at that same moment. As we pulled ourselves from it we heard a low guttural growl from behind and around us, and there in the light of the dying fire stood not just one Marshback but many, and they were mad as an Ash Cat with its tail cut off.

They are only about one to three feet tall, five to fifteen feet long, and their wings instead of being separate limbs are actually just a membrane connected to the ankle joint of the front legs that ends just before the hips, making them good for gliding but not flying. They have longer flatter snouts than other dragons, with many sharp teeth, short rough horns, and uneven bumpy spines down their backs. They are a muddy brown with moss green patches on their bodies.

The next thing we knew they were spitting at us, but it wasn't just normal spit; this was acid, and it burned through our clothes and skin, making us cry out in pain.

By then we were finished with this swamp and these thrice-cursed Marsh-backs, so we grabbed our weapons and kept them at bay as Mark was freed from his muddy grave.

He was completely unresponsive after so long under the mud, but we took him with us anyway, hoping against all odds that he wasn't gone yet. We ran and stumbled through the swamp with the dragons right behind us all the time, spitting acid at our backs to keep us moving. It felt like they were herding us like dogs do sheep.

We traveled all night, and by morning the dragons had retreated back into the swamp to follow along at a distance as we made our way out of their lands.

Tertius, 78th day of Ver.

I shall start keeping a tally now of the ones continuing on the quest, since we've lost several of the men. The men we have left are: Tobias, Frank, Tom, Steffan, Ed, Rick, and myself.

We are resting now at an inn in Emdow. We are all very thankful to be away from the swamps.

Unfortunately, Mark died before we could get him help, so we buried him just outside Emdow on the only semi-dry grassy knoll we could find, and planted a golden willow tree over his grave, saying a prayer to the gods of Light as we did.

After the many dangerous creatures he faced on Taruvek, I can't believe he died by drowning in mud. It's just not how I thought he would go.

How can we be down four men already?

In two days, after we have recovered, we will continue our journey and hunt a Timebender, one of the three great dragon breeds, and one of the most dangerous dragons in the world. A young adult has been spotted in a Nevarian forest two days' journey from us, so that is where we will go next.

Secondus, 82nd day of Ver.

We are camping tonight.

To relieve some stress and tension among the men I decided we should have a wrestling match. I went against Sir Tobias, Ed against Tom, and Frank against Rick. Steffan chose to be the judge. I won one match and Sir Tobias won one, Ed beat Tom both times, and Frank and Rick had one draw while Rick won the second round. We were all sweating and cheering each other on as we had our bouts, and by the end everyone seemed more relaxed.

Though, as we sat around the fire afterwards, there was a heavy silence as the missing members of our party were ever on our minds.

Quartus, 84th day of Ver.

We are just reaching Paldo Forest where the Timebender was seen.

Traveling through Nevar has been very enjoyable as it is a beautiful country full of rolling hills and deep, cool forests. There is a type of tree here called the Red Torch that has fiery red leaves with green veins from Ver until Cado, when the leaves turn deep gold before falling to the ground. It is spread throughout their forests like torches lighting a pathway. There are also many birds that I've never seen before. One is pink with a yellow breast and a song that puts all other birds I've heard to shame.

Sir Tobias and Steffan have been debating all day over which of the Legends was the most powerful, when Tom became exasperated and butted in, saying, "None of them were the most powerful! They all had different magic and abilities, and it's impossible to say who was the most powerful. All we know for sure is that without even one of them the Shadow Wars wouldn't have been won."

Primus, 86th day of Ver.

We are in the forest now, and it is larger than any I've seen before.

We stopped at a town called Paldo-Glen for the night, just inside the forest. The buildings are built of stone and have thatched roofs, and the town has the feel of a small village with how everyone knows everyone.

When we got there we went to the small stone temple they had built to the gods of Light, and though it was evening we said our prayers and sang a few holy songs. The priests were surprised to see us, but they, like everyone else here, were very welcoming.

It's amazing to be surrounded by so many trees at once. On Taruvek there are no forests as vast and old as this one anymore, or not yet, I suppose, since we're trying to replant them. It's like looking at endless miles of money, since our currency on Taruvek is wood strips called Rings. I can't imagine how old some of these trees are and what they'd be worth back home. The trees we use for our currency are Shard trees which have the hardest wood on Taruvek, so they last longer than any other as Rings.

Secondus, 87th day of Ver.

Last night, we got kicked out of the tavern we were staying at.

You see, Ed and Frank had a bit too much to drink and were talking about the quest, rather loudly, when they were overheard by some of the men in the tavern who didn't like what they were saying.

Tobias and I were on the other side of the room by the fireplace, when I saw and heard what was happening. I said a prayer that they'd handle it wisely and say they were speculating or something like that, but then Frank opened his big mouth and loudly proclaimed, "Before we're through with this quest, I will cook up some dragon steaks and have them for dinner!"

Ed then had the bright idea to chime in and say, "And I will become known as the best tracker in the world after I track down and kill the dragons for him to cook."

As I heard this I could only bury my face in my hands and shake my head in misery.

Their words tipped the men over the edge and fists started to fly, as well as mugs, bottles, and chairs.

Tom, of course, loves a good fight and jumped right into the fray with gusto. Tobias groaned beside me just before I heard a loud crash and finally looked up from my hands to see what made him groan. Tom and Ed had grabbed a table and were charging through the room knocking down men, tables, and chairs as they went.

I buried my face again and said to Tobias, "Tell me when it's over."

Once it was finally over, we had to pay a large amount of money for the damages, and we were thrown out with all our packs and banned from the tavern.

We're on the road again now, and all of us are yawning because we didn't sleep well in the streets.

Unfortunately, we haven't seen any signs of the Timebender yet.

Tertius, 88th day of Ver.

Today we heard it!

The young Timebender roared its victory over its prey. We found where it killed an animal half an hour later, but it was gone by then, as was its food. The tracks left behind were definitely from a smaller Timebender, not yet fully grown. We shall keep on this path and hope we catch it soon.

If the dragon is a male we will have to shield our eyes from the bright light they can make with the black veils we bought at a village on the journey here, and we'll need to be careful to watch for time to speed up by watching our hourglass at all times. If it's a female we will need all our lanterns to be lit to have any hope of seeing through the absolute darkness they can cause, and we'll need to watch for the sand in the hourglass to slow.

All our bug bites and acid burns are gone now, and the last hunt is slowly fading from memory. Even if the death of our friends isn't.

Quartus, 89th day of Ver.

We found her!

From the descriptions I've heard of this type of dragon, an amethyst colored Timebender with opal spikes is a female, while ruby with pearl spikes would be a male. Her scales sparkled in the dappled sunlight as she turned to look at us, and her eyes were like living opals shining back at us with all the knowledge of time in them even at her young age. I froze, feeling like she was seeing into my past and judging the kind of man I was in that moment.

After a minute I shook myself out of my reverie, wondering as I did why she wasn't attacking us. Remembering our plan I quickly lit my lantern, and cocked my harpoon gun. Hopefully the others would remember their lanterns too, and Tobias the hourglass.

Before they could make a move, though, her eyes hardened at the click my gun made, and then darkness enveloped us. My lantern flickered but stayed lit, thankfully.

We stood in a circle with our swords and harpoon guns drawn, trying to see into the depths of the darkness by the light of the one lantern.

She struck then, plowing through our ranks like we were no more than saplings in her way. Frank got stepped on, and Sir Tobias got knocked out by her tail before she disappeared into the darkness again. My lantern thankfully didn't break when I fell, so I held it up high again as we regrouped, surrounding our injured members.

When she struck again, it was just with her tail sweeping several of the men off their feet. I leapt over it as it came at my legs and shot my harpoon gun into the darkness where her body should be, but I could feel and hear my harpoon hit a tree instead, so I cut the line.

Ed was stabbed in the leg by one of the sharp spikes when she swept him off his feet, and he lay bleeding on the ground.

Then something bizarre happened. It was as if we all blacked out at once, and then woke up at once because when we did the darkness had dissipated and she was gone, leaving us all laying on our backs with no idea what had happened. I can only assume she slowed time down to make her escape, but since Tobias had been knocked out and dropped the hourglass, we couldn't be sure.

With three men injured, we could not continue the hunt. Steffan treated them as best he could, and we began the trek back out of the forest.

After it happened, Rick had the audacity to say, "Did she seem…I don't know, intelligent to you guys? Like she intentionally didn't kill us even though she easily could have? It makes me wonder if there may be some truth to the stories we've heard about them."

I immediately said, "Of course she wasn't intelligent! Did you hear her talk to us? No! She tried to escape because she was clearly outnumbered."

What I didn't tell him was that the same thought had briefly crossed my mind too, but I knew it couldn't be so.

Quintus, 90th day of Ver.

We stopped at an inn along the road for the night and while there, we drank to our friends and said a prayer to the gods of Light. As we sat there we remembered the good times we had with them. Joe was always finding a new sweetheart, Charles had a wife but no children and was passionate about the elk herd he'd been breeding for almost two decades, and Mark was always going hunting and thus hadn't married because he was never at home. They would be remembered fondly by all of us and their families back home.

Quintus, 95th day of Ver.

Our luck here on Kelasinar has been terrible.

We have not killed a single dragon yet, nor even managed to injure one. We have nothing to show for our efforts, except death. But for their deaths to mean something we must try to fulfill our quest, otherwise they will have died for naught.

So now we are on our way to Pali, the Daln port of Nevar to board a ship headed for the hot jungle continent of Dalnar. There we will hunt the Leafwelders, Stormrenders, Sanddiggers, and Metalbreaths. And maybe, just maybe, our luck will be better.

DALNAR

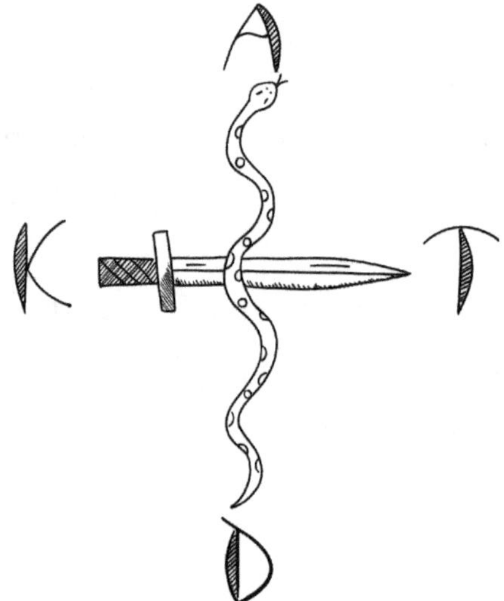

Quintus, 100th day of Ver.

We have set sail for Dalnar at last.

The ship we are sailing on is not made of metal or steam-powered like our Taruveken ships; instead it has great white sails to catch the wind, and they even have a Galewing and Rider on board to keep us going, even when there's no wind. With their help it will take us four weeks to sail there.

In the meantime we shall enjoy a rest, and the sunshine of the Daln ocean, while I try to keep my men from killing the Galewing. After all, we're only after wild ones, while this one has a Rider, so we must not kill it.

We sent a letter home with a ship sailing to Taruvek to give to the family of Mark. Death is the unfortunate risk we take on a great quest such as this.

Quintus, 110th day of Ver.

The heat is becoming oppressive as we sail ever farther Daln. The Galewing Rider and his dragon use their power to keep a cool breeze blowing on us during the heat of the day, but I'm not sure we can bear this much longer. The humidity makes it hard to breathe, and sweat is our constant companion day and night.

We're also incredibly bored, as there is not much to do. We've sparred and practiced as much as we can, but the heat and humidity force us to stop not long after starting.

Instead we have begun planning how we can kill the next dragons on our list. Without Mark, our expert on hunting dangerous animals, I worry our plans won't be as good, but we shall have to do our best without him.

We will start with the Sanddigger, as it's called, since it's only going to get hotter and we want to get the worst part over with. Our plan is to find the burrow of one, then lure it out, and as it exits its burrow we will attack it with everything we have. Ed suggested we dump oil in the burrow and light it on fire, but that would ruin the head, so that idea won't work. We're still coming up with our plans for hunting the Stormrender, the Leafwelder, and the Metalbreath dragons. Frank threw out the idea of attracting the Leafwelder with its favorite foods, which I think could work. We'll keep discussing it as we travel.

Secundus, 122nd day of Ver.

We're in Dalnar at last!

We hit some storms that delayed us by a few days, but other than that the trip went smoothly.

The people here are beautiful in their resemblance to the jungles they call home, with their dark skin the color of the rich brown bark of the magnificent trees, thick, red or auburn hair like the leaves in Cado, and blue or violet eyes like the shade-loving flowers that grow in abundance here.

Their buildings are built on stilts or in the trees due to the flooding this area often gets, being so close to the ocean.

It is unbearably hot and humid still, but they tell us we'll acclimate to it soon enough. I truly hope they're right.

Unfortunately dragons aren't very common here, so we must be careful of the questions we ask as we search for our prey so we don't raise suspicions among the tribes here.

Quartus, 124th day of Ver.

Tomorrow is the last day of the month of Ver, then the month of Aestas begins, and the real heat will be upon us.

We've begun our journey into the Veliku Desert, which stretches along one side of the continent, to hunt the fastest dragon on land, the Sanddigger. We are going to the great white sand flats at the edge of the dunes, where they are said to hunt the herds of camels that roam there. We shall travel through the oasis on our way to the white sand flats.

Quintus, 125the day of Ver.

We've reached the Fraevuw Oasis, where the Glass Palace is.

As we approached it I could hardly believe what I was seeing could be real.

The palace sits on the island in the middle of the Split River, surrounded by lush green trees and gardens. The city on the banks of both sides of the river sprawls out in every direction for as far as the green of the oasis does.

The Glass Palace is like a crystalline rainbow shining in the light of the desert sun. The walls and roofs are all different colors of glass, and the windows are the only clear glass on the whole thing.

According to the locals, the glass is made by Sanddiggers and their Riders in a large factory nearby. Sand is brought from every part of the continent to create different types and colors of glass, and then the Metalbreaths and their Riders create the frames for the glass. So even though it is created solely of glass and dragon metal, the palace is much stronger than you can imagine.

The glass industry of this province of Dalnar is the biggest revenue of trade they have.

As we got closer to the city, I couldn't take my eyes off of the palace. Even the bridges that cross the river to the island it sits on are made of glass, each one a different color.

I was pulled from my reverie when the guard at the gate asked for our names and purpose in the city. I told him the same story I told the Kelasinarians about us writing this book, and thankfully he bought it and even pointed us towards a good inn, The Crystal Flagon, to stay the night. Seems glass is extremely common here and is used in every possible way. We ordered our food, and paid in advance for rooms and baths to wash the desert off of our bodies. The food is flavored with foreign spices native to Dalnar, and it is absolutely delicious. I almost wish we could stay here longer.

Primus, 1st day of Aestas.

It has been a day and a half since we left the oasis, and here I thought we had experienced the hottest place in this world already, but the Kelasinarian desert was nothing compared to the Dalnarian one.

We finally saw a Sanddigger in the distance. At least I think we did… It was so brief, and the sun was so bright on the golden sands, that it was hard to tell for sure. But Tom, Rick, and I saw it gliding between the dunes as we traveled through the flats along them. By the time we got to the area where we saw it, it was gone. It was the same golden color as the sand, but it shimmered and sparkled more like citrine. It has a broad head and a shovel-like tail. It looks built for running not flying, even its wings are an example of this as they are short and deep made for gliding low instead of flying high. An interesting thing the Sanddigger can do is it can create glass shards by collecting sand in a pouch beneath its chin, and then as it breathes a short burst of hot plasma, it sprays the sand through it, creating glass.

We are searching the sand diligently for any signs of a burrow. Surely they must leave some piles or something when they bury themselves.

Tertius, 3rd day of Aestas.

We came upon it unexpectedly today.

Rick actually stepped on it, and as he did, it burst out of the sand and bit his leg.

We all drew our weapons and started to charge it together, but it whipped sand into half the men's eyes with its tail, then sprayed the rest of us with shards of sharp glass.

We all cried out as the glass cut us, and sand got into their eyes. In a flash, it lunged at those it had sprayed with glass and plowed into them with its broad head before darting through their midst and slamming its heavy shovel-tipped tail into the chest of Ed as it did. In moments, it was gone as it sped across the sands.

As we pulled ourselves together and assessed our injuries it became apparent that Rick's leg was bleeding badly, and Ed was unconscious with several broken ribs and possibly a punctured lung.

Most of the rest of us are cut and bleeding from the Sanddigger's glass and bruised from it ramming us with its hard head but we can still walk.

So we have made two stretchers, and are headed back towards the nearest town on the map. Hopefully we will make it there before it's too late for Rick and Ed...

Quartus, 4th day of Aestas.

Both men have pulled through, but Rick's leg injury is bad; even so, he is determined to continue on our quest. He says he's never failed a mission and he won't fail this one, either. Thankfully Ed only has a few broken ribs, not a punctured lung, and he can continue on with us as well.

We are restocking in the port town of Felod, and then we shall go on to hunt the Stormrenders that fly along the coast. Hopefully we will have better luck with this one than we have had with the others.

Primus, 6th day of Aestas.

We've been traveling along the coast for a few days now.

Apparently rain is a sign of a Stormrender nearby, but because it naturally rains daily here, I have no idea how to find one.

Stormrenders don't have territories or certain habitats like other varieties; instead they fly with the storms, absorbing lightning as they go. These dragons are the fastest flyers of all dragons, and they are as erratic as the storms they love. They can be different shades of gray, lightning-colored, or the dull purple color like the sky gets before a bad storm. Their eyes are neon green with gray flecks, and their wings have lightning bolt patterns on them.

Our plan for killing this one was hard to come up with, since it flies with the storms and doesn't land often. But the best we could come up with is to wait for a storm to come, set up all of our harpoon guns on a cliff, and wait for a Stormrender to fly by before shooting it and reeling it in as best we can to kill it.

Quartus, 9th day of Aestas.

As we rounded a bend in the cliff along the coast, we unexpectedly found an adult Stormrender eating its recent kill.

At first we all just stood there with it looking at us and us at it, too shocked to react. Then everyone was scrambling for their weapons and it was summoning its storm magic. Thankfully it could only do one lightning bolt every few minutes and only if it had flown in a storm recently.

Just then a bolt of lightning struck out of nowhere, hitting Steffan, killing him instantly as he raised his arms up in a futile attempt to block it. He lit up like a pillar of light for a moment, the electricity from the lightning dancing across his body.

The thunder from it boomed so loudly it knocked some of us down and made our ears ring, even as the electricity made our hair stand on end. While we were momentarily stunned, the Stormrender called forth hail and a deluge of rain on us. The hailstones were the size of my fist, and one knocked Sir Tobias out completely while the rest of us were beaten and bruised.

We protected our heads by holding our cloaks up taut above us, and the cunning Stormrender took the opportunity to sweep the lot of us off our feet with its tail before taking off and flying away with all the speed of the lightning it had just summoned.

As soon as it was out of sight, the hail and rain stopped, and we were able to climb up off the ground from beneath our shields.

We looked like we got into a bar fight and lost with how bruised and bloodied we were from the hail. Sir Tobias looks especially bad with his head wound bleeding profusely and all the bruises he received from being unprotected from the hail the entire time.

It is unlikely he will be the same when he wakes up, especially since this isn't his first head injury on this trip.

Unfortunately we could not take Steffan's charred body with us, so we said a prayer as we buried him at the edge of the forest on the coast, planting a red beacon tree over his body to forever shine out over the sea with its bright yellow-orange leaves. At least his final resting place is a beautiful one.

I dread the day we return and I must tell each of the families of these men what happened to their loved ones. I'm not sure what we will do without Steffan's healing knowledge.

How can we be failing so miserably when we are so much more intelligent than dragons? Have we misjudged the dragons?

Primus, 11th day of Aestas.

Sir Tobias woke up finally just as we reached the village of Tafol, but just as we feared he was not the same. Seems he doesn't recognize any of us, and he won't calm down. The healer of the town had to give him a sleeping draught so she could tend to his wounds. He will have to return to Taruvek to heal fully. We have given up on hunting the Stormrender, and some of the men were close to giving up on the quest completely, but I convinced them we must honor our friends and bring at least one dragon head home.

Tertius, 13th day of Aestas.

Men left: Frank, Ed, Rick, Tom, and me.

Our next prey is the Leafwelder, which should be easy since it's the smallest type of dragon in all of the world at only six inches to five feet tall, two to ten feet long, and with a wing span of three to fifteen feet.

Problem is, these little guys are impossible to find unless they wish to be found. It's said they like berries and mushrooms, so we bought a bunch of those at the last town to leave out by our campsite at night. Hopefully they will draw one out of hiding.

Quartus, 19th day of Aestas.

Six days.

Six days we've been searching for the Leafwelder. Six days we've been leaving goodies out. And for six days we've seen nothing.

I don't understand why it's not working. It should have by now. We are becoming more and more discouraged, and even Tom, the life of the party, isn't in a good mood.

The forest we are traveling through is dense and full of all manner of deadly creatures. Even some of the plants are predators of certain creatures.

Thankfully none of them move like the Ash Trees of Taruvek though; those trees give me nightmares. The tales say that if you fall asleep too close to one it will slowly move over you until you cannot escape, and then it consumes you alive.

Secundus, 22nd day of Aestas.

We finally caught a Leafwelder this morning!

It has been stealing the goodies laid out for it in the dead of night, so last night we set a snare to catch it, and it worked! But she was none too happy about that. I could tell she was a female because she had no horns, while males have a small pair of curved horns. She looked to be mid-sized at about two feet tall, five feet long, with a ten foot wingspan.

We were up and grabbing our harpoon guns immediately, but before we could get a shot off, another Leafwelder swooped in at us, this one a male and a good foot bigger than her in height. His peridot green eyes were filled with fury as he saw his mate stuck in the snare. Moments later, the camp was filled with screeching and claws as five young Leafwelders filled the air, swooping and scratching at us.

For about a minute, chaos erupted all around me as we swatted at the small menaces filling the air. As quickly as it started, though, it ended, because the female chewed through the rope around her leg and leapt into the air with a throaty growl, calling for her family to follow her into the jungle. As they flew off, their iridescent green-brown scales sparkled in the dim light of the morning before they vanished, as if they had never been there.

We all stood for a minute panting, blood dripping from the tiny scratches that covered our bare arms, necks, and faces. The male dragon had given me a scratch running from my hairline to my chin on the right side of my face, and I could feel that it was deep enough to leave a long thin scar.

I couldn't believe what had just happened. It was humiliating to be beaten by a swarm of tiny dragons.

As we collected our wits and started cleaning ourselves up, we decided that we should try to track them and find their nest to bring the whole family back to Taruvek to mount their heads on our walls.

Quartus, 24th day of Aestas.

We never found their nest, but the male and female found us early this morning while we slept.

We woke to their screeching as they swooped down from the trees at us where we lay, and they started spraying their gas all over the camp. Unfortunately it seems all the berries and mushrooms we had been leaving out are especially good for inducing sleep when turned into a gas.

Rick grabbed his harpoon gun and, while holding his breath, fired a shot at the female, but he missed as she dodged. The male gave a guttural growl of anger as he saw this and swooped down, landing on Rick's chest and knocking him onto his back, but instead of biting him like I thought he would, he breathed the sleeping gas into Rick's face, making him go unconscious immediately. As the female flew towards me, after gassing the others, I quickly put the blanket over my head and held my breath. I felt her claws brush the blanket as she passed over me. Even under the blanket I could feel the gas making me tired. I didn't fall asleep like the others had, but it was several minutes before I could come out from under the blanket. When I did, the dragons were gone, and the gas had dissipated. The sun was just beginning to light the sky as most of the men were just beginning to stir after having been asleep, their eyes and faces were red and puffy. Rick was completely unconscious and nothing we did would wake him up. His face, throat, and eyes were very red and swollen, and we could only hope he would pull through.

After this attack, and with Rick's condition, we have decided to leave this area of the jungle and the Leafwelders in it behind.

Quintus, 25th day of Aestas.

We made it to a village named Kesil in the territory of Razidaln, deep in the forest.

The people here live in houses built in the trees, which for most of us is a bit disconcerting to traverse, but they walk the thin bridges without fear.

Apparently a Dragon Caretaker, who is also a Legend from the Shadow Wars, has heard about us somehow; we saw her and several dragons that were with her. Ed heard her asking about us in the village. I don't know how she knows what we're doing, but she does. Ed immediately came and found us at the inn, and we packed up and snuck out the back before she came. We are now on the road again and trying to move quickly.

On the bright side, Rick has finally woken up, but the swelling in his face and neck is still going down. He says he dreamt of trees and giant squirrels the whole time he was unconscious, and the squirrels kept throwing fist-sized nuts at his head. I think he may have some mental trauma from his ordeal.

He also won't stop insisting that the legends about dragons must have some truth to them. I think this is a side effect from the gas the dragon released in his face.

Secondus, 27th day of Aestas.

Rick's swelling is gone now, though he shrieks every time a squirrel crosses our path. It's disconcerting to see my friend, an ex-spy, so scared of such a small creature. I truly wonder how terrible his hallucinations were from that gas.

We are heading towards the home of the Metalbreaths; the Silver Mountains.

It is said there are statues of animals and even a few people up there, created by their liquid metal breath. I suppose we shall see for ourselves soon.

We are riding what they call thorn-tusked elephants through the rainforest. They are terribly difficult to mount with their great height, they have a gait that rocks you like one of the rocking chairs on Kelasinar, and they are quite slow compared to the horse steeds Kelasinar uses and the elk steeds of Taruvek. I wonder what type of mount the last continent, Arrovad, has.

Tertius, 28th day of Aestas.

We had to camp on the forest floor last night.

Most of our trip through these jungles we've come to waystations in the trees placed strategically for travelers to sleep in between towns, but this close to the Silver Mountains there are none. I now understand why the people of this continent choose to live in the trees.

We were up all night warding off forest cats and wood yotes, which are similar to coyotes but longer, dark brown, and with glowing green eyes. Not to mention all the venomous snakes and bugs that are active on the forest floor at night. We even saw the enormous Titanaboa slithering along between the great trunks. Thank the Lights it wasn't hungry. Apparently the warriors of some of the tribes ride these massive snakes into battle, like we ride the Irishean bull elk on Taruvek.

Needless to say, we are not in good moods this morning. Though the hot drink Frank learned to make from the locals in the last town did help to lift our gloom a little. Apparently they call it cocoa coffee.

Quintus, 30th day of Aestas.

We've reached the Silver Mountains, and though they aren't as magnificent as Kelasinar's Dividing Mountains, or as huge as Taruvek's Pengar Mountains, they are still breathtaking in their own right. They stretch for the sky in thin gray peaks, like teeth coming out of the ground. The forest floor is growing more and more rocky as we approach them, so we had to leave our guide and the elephants behind.

Primus, 31st day of Aestas.

The remaining men and I have climbed our way up into the mountains now, and we just saw the first statue. It was a large Stone Cat native to Dalnar, and based on its crouched position, it must have been attacking a dragon's baby or something, because it is solid metal now.

According to the locals, dragon metal is the hardest metal in the world, but it can only be forged into weapons and tools by a Metalbreath and its Rider.

When we face one, we must avoid its liquid metal at all costs.

Tertius, 33rd day of Aestas.

We've stumbled upon an old Metalbreath nest. The shells from the eggs are nearly as hard as dragon metal. The young dragonets must have an incredibly powerful egg tooth to break through that shell. Around the nest are animal bones and more metal statues, almost as if the mother dragon was decorating her nesting area.

Quintus, 35th day of Aestas.

After we reached a high mountain valley, we saw our first Metalbreath in the distance.

It was a copper colored one. Metalbreath scales are harder than any other dragon's, and this one looked to be the biggest size they can get at fifteen feet tall, twenty-one feet long, and with a forty-two foot wingspan. It spotted us and flew into the mountains before we could get close enough to shoot at it. We'll continue after it and hopefully catch it soon.

Many ideas were thrown around about how we should kill it, from attracting it with food like we've tried before, to setting up a rock slide, and even melting down the metal statues and killing it with its own liquid metal. We could not all agree on a plan though, so it's been decided that we will just wing it with this one and see how that goes. The only thing we know for sure is that we must all have the expensive diamond-tipped harpoon bolts and swords we bought ready at all times, as they are the only things that can pierce their scales.

Primus, 36th day of Aestas.

We caught up to it at last!

It was dozing in a cave, and we startled it awake as our footsteps echoed throughout the cavern. It roared its fury at us, which was deafeningly loud in the cave. The men and I circled it and went to attack, but suddenly there was a second one coming at us from the entrance of the cave, this one silver in color.

We ended up back-to-back with each other as the two dragons growled. Then just as one opened its mouth and breathed its liquid metal at us, Tom pointed ahead and yelled, "Quick, into the tunnel!" But even as he started for the back of the cave, Ed's hand was hit by the liquid metal, and he cried out in pain as he was burned.

Frank grabbed him and dragged him along with us as we ran into the tunnel. Unfortunately, it was downhill a little ways and the two Metalbreaths poured as much liquid metal into the tunnel as they could, which began to run down the stone pathway.

Tom yelled at us again in a panicked voice, this time telling everyone that we needed to run faster or he'd have metal feet.

Secondus, 37th day of Aestas.

Unfortunately, Tom did end up stepping in some of the metal as it rushed down the tunnel after us, but it stayed just on his boot. We'll need a diamond-tipped tool to chisel the metal and free him from his boot, which has completely hardened around his foot, making him limp along with a loud clang every step. Ed's hand is now basically a metal club. Sadly nothing can be done for him now that it has hardened over his burned flesh. It pains him greatly because of the burn beneath it, but at least dragon metal is sterile, so he shouldn't develop an infection.

We wandered the cave for a few hours before finally finding our way to an opening and escaping. By then it was nighttime, and the creatures of the forest were awake and active including some of the predators. We ended up camping just inside the cave and lighting a fire to ward off some of the bugs and creatures. It was far too hot out to actually enjoy the heat of the fire, though.

Quartus, 39th day of Aestas.

We got lost on our way back to our guide.

Thankfully we brought a map, but this accursed forest looks the same no matter which direction you face, especially since you can't see the sun clearly through the dense foliage.

Frank had to climb a tree to see which way the sun was rising, and finally we had a heading to travel by. Three more times one of us had to climb a tree to figure out which way to go.

We finally found a town called Eblu by nightfall and got rooms at an inn. Fortunately a smith here had some diamond-tipped chisels, so Tom has been freed from his boot and is keeping it as a souvenir.

Before we could settle into our rooms at the inn, though, the Dragon Caretaker appeared again. This time, Rick saw her from the window of the inn, and we quickly snuck out the back and made a run for it.

Quintus, 40th day of Aestas.

We are heading towards the port town of Sea-Fare, which we should reach sometime tomorrow. We are in a more populated area of the jungle, and as we go we have passed several treehouse towns and villages. The styles they build them in vary as much as the trees themselves; some are round, others boxy, and some A-framed. The colors of the wood they're built out of varies by region too, and the people have windows of every color of glass imaginable. We cannot stop in any of them though, for fear of the Caretaker Ilaria, as she's called, catching up to us with her horde of dragons.

As we travel, Tom sings us the different ballads he's learned in the taverns and inns of Kelasinar and Dalnar, many of them are about the Legends of the Shadow Wars before they became Legends, when they were starting their fight against the gods of Shadow. The songs seem to help keep Rick distracted, though a few times he's spotted a squirrel and nearly leapt from his elephant, but we have Frank riding with him, and he's caught him each time.

Primus, 41st day of Aetsas.

Seems we've failed yet again to kill any of our prey, and with the Caretaker hunting us down, it is time to leave this continent.

Ed and Rick are leaving us to go back home. Ed with his metal hand won't be much good in a fight anymore, plus he was injured by the Timebender and Sanddigger before this, so he is ready to be done. And Rick is still traumatized from his experience with the Leafwelder, and he's still recovering from the injury he received from the Sanddigger. He said he can't continue and be helpful on the quest, so for our sake he must leave.

Frank, Tom, and I will sail to Arrovad to hunt the final dragons on our list. I hope we can get at least one before we go back home to Taruvek.

Since it is Primus, we stopped at a temple of the Seven gods of Light at midday and said our prayers to them with all the Dalnarian followers. The temples here are made of glass and beautifully stained wood carved into amazing designs. I truly think the gods of Light must have designed these temples themselves, for there are none like them in all the world. As I sang the Dalnarian holy songs, I was in awe of the rich beautiful voices of the people native to this land.

I never would have seen the beauty of these continents and their people were it not for this quest, so at least one good thing has come of it so far.

ARROVAD

Primus, 51st day of Aestas.

We've been sailing for nearly two weeks now, and the temperature is steadily dropping as we get farther Arro. It will be another six weeks before we reach Arrovad. I hope we can stay sane during that time on the ship.

Our ship is Dalnarian, which means it's made of wood and is powered by a team of strong foot pedalers who power the large paddle at the back.

The sea creatures we've seen as we sail have been truly amazing. We saw a hippocampus off in the distance, a pod of double-humped white whales, some antlered seals, and a family of two-tusked narwhals which almost capsized us. According to an old Dalnarian sailor, narwhals hold special significance to some people as they represent a major life-changing moment coming to the person who sees them first, which in this case was me. I wonder what that could mean for me...

On Arrovad, the final continent of our quest, we will be hunting the Frostcreeper, the Tidebringer, and the Soulreader. The last one is said to be the most dangerous dragon of all, even more so than the great Astroweaver of outer space, but from what facts I've pulled from the many legends about them, they seem to be the most gentle dragon, as they don't even eat meat.

Tertius, 68th day of Aestas.

I hate the ocean.

Quintus, 70th day of Aestas.

The endless pitching and tossing, pitching and tossing, pitching and tossing, has worn me out. Even on calm days, it's still rocking.

And don't even get me started on the storms that rage out on the open ocean, or the food we've had to eat for the last many weeks. Here I thought the trip from Kelasinar to Dalnar was hard. I truly had no idea men could survive such things for so long.

Thankfully the captain and crew of the ship we're on are quite experienced, otherwise we would have perished long ago.

Tertius, 83rd day of Aestas.

We have at long last reached the archipelago continent of Arrovad!

I have never seen such a vast number of islands. Around, between, and connecting the islands are floating homes, bridges, and cities.

The islands themselves are only used for growing and raising enough food for all the people. The days here are incredibly long and the sun does not set this time of year. I hope we can sleep with the sun shining on us even at night.

The people of Arrovad are very stark in contrast to the people of Dalnar. They have very pale ivory skin, white, silver, or blue-black hair; and eyes that can be as light as sand or the darkest richest brown you can imagine. Their hair is also very fine and silky compared to the thick, curlier, red hair of the Dalnarians. They are taller than any of the other people we've seen but still very strong. They exude a certain gracefulness in their movements that makes me think they could either dance or fight extremely well, maybe even both at once. Overall, their appearance reminds me of tall mountains touched by the first snows of Hiems, but their eyes hold all the warmth of Aestas in their deep brown depths.

Oh, and they ride massive Snow Bears here, the very thought of which honestly terrifies me a bit.

Quartus, 84th of Aestas.

Froast Haveen, the town we are staying in for the night, is so amazing!

The buildings and homes are all circular domes of varying sizes built on a wood platform with walls of thick plaster which are covered on the outside with gems. The windows in the domes are made of diamond, and at the very top of each one is a large diamond window to let lots of light in during the day, these windows also serve to reflect the bioluminescent squid ink lanterns they use all winter long. Each dome has an open pit in the center that allows access to the water below; over this pit is a hand crank like you'd use over a well, and they use sealed pots made of gems that they put their food in and lower down to the hydrothermal vents to cook their food. These hydrothermal vents are everywhere under the water between the islands, and are actually fairly close to the surface in some places, thus the hot water not only cooks their food, but helps heat their homes through the long dark winters. The waterways above and close to the vents never freeze over even during the coldest nights. Each home is just one big room with curtained off sections to serve as bedrooms.

The palace of each country is built over the highest concentration of vents around their islands, and thus it has many more domes all connected by covered walkways.

Secondus, 87th day of Aestas.

We are finally on the wild islands where the dragons live.

They intentionally have left these three large islands and the many small ones around them untouched for forests, wildlife, and dragons to thrive on. We had to bribe the ferryman handsomely to bring us here, as it's restricted to protect the bit of wilderness and wildlife they have left.

The forests on these islands are different. The pines are tall and thin like the people, the bark is silvery-gray, the needles are a blue-green color, and the pinecones are as big as my head and black. The strangest thing is, it's silent. As if every living creature here is holding its breath for something. It's like they all know why we're here.

Quintus, 90th day of Aestas.

Yesterday, we felt the first signs of a Frostcreeper as the temperature dropped significantly upon us entering its territory. The nights are starting to get colder already, but we're feeling the frigid temperatures even during the day, and it is much more extreme than it should be this time of Aestas. This makes me think we are getting closer to our prey.

When we find one we will need to incapacitate it as quickly as possible, as there are only three of us left to kill it. We've bought some large barbed spears to fight it with. Our plan is to kill a caribou, set up the large net we still have from Kelasinar up in the air above the carcass, and drop it on the Frostcreeper when it comes.

Secondus, 92nd day of Aestas.

We found more signs of a Frostcreeper, but we have been unsuccessful in finding it. I think this particular Frostcreeper is hiding from us. We have found footprints in the dirt, ice pillars, and areas with evidence of its frost blast where it might have caught prey.

We heard it roar for the first time while we walked, and it sounded like ice cracking and an avalanche happening at the same time. It sent a shiver down my spine to hear it.

Quintus, 95th day of Aestas.

It's getting even colder, and I now think we're being followed by the Frostcreeper.

We are getting frostbite from how extreme the cold is, especially at night. We weren't prepared for such temperatures in Aestas. I don't know how the people here survive Hiems when it is dark and cold.

Primus, 96th day of Aestas.

The trap worked this time, but Tom is dead.

We were lying in wait with a rope to drop the net on the dragon, the caribou dead beneath it. The temperature was continuing to drop by the minute, and we were all shivering uncontrollably. Then it appeared walking through the trees, frost crawling over the ground all around it like a moving carpet. It took my breath away to look at it, the scales sparkled in the shadowed light like a million diamonds. Snow-white wings had the swirling patterns of frost on their surface, and aquamarine eyes glowed with a cold light. It was like looking at living gems.

As soon as it stepped beneath the net, Tom released it to fall upon the dragon. A roar of icy fury filled the air, then those frigid aquamarine eyes fell upon me and Frank, and I felt the temperature drop drastically. Even as that happened, it blasted us with frost, which gave us instant frostbite on the exposed parts of our bodies. I almost felt like my body was freezing to the ground I was laying on.

The net didn't slow it or restrict it as much as we hoped, and so it turned towards Tom next, and even as he swung his sword at it, the blade stopped inches from the dragon's neck when it concentrated a blast of pure ice at him until he froze solid.

The unthinkable happened then. It spun to fight Frank and I again, stumbling a little when it stepped on the net, and as it did it bumped the ice statue that was Tom over onto the rocks that were all around us, and he shattered.

Seeing the horror on our faces as we watched our friend shatter, it struggled out of the net and sprang straight up into the air, disappearing above the pines.

We peeled ourselves up off the ground, and went to silently gather the pieces of Tom up. We couldn't find his left hand no matter how hard and long we searched for it.

I never knew a man could die like that. I almost feel like I shattered with him as I looked at the pieces. I felt so broken over the deaths of so many of my friends. How could we have gone so far together for it to end like this for him?

Quartus, 99th day of Aestas.

Men left: Frank and me.

We've made a sort of temporary campsite in the forest while we recover from the Frostcreeper encounter. We buried the pieces of Tom in a small clearing, planting a stony pine above him. Frank has lost all motivation to hunt the last dragons, and his cooking has gotten really bad. He keeps talking about leaving for Taruvek, but I've convinced him we can't yet, not without at least trying to hunt the Tidebringer and Soulreader, so that this quest won't end as a complete failure.

We will go to the rocky shoreline tomorrow to hunt for a Tidebringer. Hopefully we find it quickly.

Primus, 101st day of Aestas.

We've found one!

It's a grand old sapphire-colored Ocean-Tidebringer, meaning it's the biggest they get. We came upon it quite accidentally yesterday and have been trying to come up with a plan ever since. We've been watching it, and all it does is sleep. There seems to be a small whale carcass nearby recently picked clean.

Seems old dragons take long naps after gorging themselves. Tomorrow we will sneak up on it, and attack it from both directions at once. This will give us the best chance of killing it with only two of us attacking it. That way, if it wakes up, one of us will distract it while the other sneaks up behind it and kills it.

Secondus, 102nd day of Aestas.

Frank and I attacked it at the same time.

Of course it picked that moment to roll over and sneeze out boiling hot snot right on Frank, making him cry out in pain as the boiling goop ran down his face and body. After it sneezed on him, he couldn't see much or dive out of the way, so as its big head came down from sneezing it landed right on him as. Even as I saw him get trapped beneath its head, I got caught under its belly as it rolled over a little.

I waited a few minutes to be sure it hadn't woken up; then I wriggled free of its girth, and snuck to its head to see if Frank was still alive.

He unfortunately didn't make it, and all I could see of him was his feet. I said a prayer to the gods of Light, and then snuck back into the forest.

Quintus, 105th day of Aestas.

I've been wandering the forest aimlessly for a while reflecting on all my friends that have been lost or injured on this quest. And yet I have nothing to show for it. They died for nothing. I feel guilty for their deaths. This whole quest was my idea, and I convinced each of them to come along.

Night is coming, and though it doesn't get dark here this time of year, creatures still come out of hiding when the temperature starts to drop. I need to find a safe place to hide, as I no longer have someone to watch my back. The quiet of the forest makes my spine tingle and my heart race as if there are eyes on me, but when I look around I see nothing but endless trees. I can't help but feel like death awaits me behind every one.

If I can just make it back to the shore where we were dropped off, I can signal the ferryman to come get me.

Primus, 106th day of Aestas.

Last night I barely slept.

I had to keep my fire burning all night or risk having some wild animal attack me.

At one point I was nodding off when I heard a great growl from close by. I jerked awake and raised my harpoon gun, fearing it may be a Snow Bear, which are common on these islands and are hunting and eating as much as they can before the dark cold truly begins.

After a moment the growl came again, and I realized it was my stomach. I'm nearly out of food now since Frank was carrying most of it while I carried the other supplies. What food I am carrying, I have no idea how to cook, nor do I have any pots to cook it with. So I've been eating uncooked potatoes and rice.

The plants here are very different from those back home on Taruvek, so I don't know what's edible and what's potentially deadly.

Tertius, 108th day of Aestas.

I'm officially lost.

I can't even seem to find my way to the shore, let alone the spot where we landed. I don't even know if I'm on the right island anymore because we crossed a sandbar to two different ones while we traveled, and they seem to all look the same. Plus, I don't have the sun to guide me since it doesn't set.

I have one more meal left, and that's after rationing it. I made the mistake of eating a deep purple berry I found, and my stomach rebelled against me the rest of the day.

This may be the way I die. Lost, alone, and hungry in a forest far from home. I suppose it's a just punishment for what I've done.

As I lay here I planted the last two tree seeds, one for Frank and the other for me. Frank's seed is for a jade pine, mine is for a purple aspen. Maybe one day someone will find these trees, and my body and this journal beneath them, and we will be remembered.

I am beginning to wonder if maybe dragons are smarter than I first thought...

Primus, 111th day of Aestas.

A Soulreader found me.

She is just as the stories told, gentle and wise. She has soft light brown fur, with a silver mane running down her spine to the tip of her tail, small round ears, and metallic silver scales on her feet. Her four light brown wings are feathered with a few silver ones shimmering throughout them. But it was her eyes that held me transfixed as she approached me slowly where I sat slumped against a silver pine tree with little will to live. They were gentle and soft like a doe's eyes, but a richer brown with silver flecks that sparkled like glass in the dappled sunlight.

I lay there frozen in awe and fear, for as she looked into my eyes I felt her very soul brush mine.

She spoke to me through her mind in a quiet gentle voice, saying, *"So you're the one hunting dragons. I've felt the disquiet of the forest from the moment you entered it."* She paused, and when I said nothing she continued, *"You've failed your quest, lost your companions, and now lost the will to live. But you have not come through all this without learning something, have you?"*

I tried to speak, but I had to clear my throat to get anything out; so shocked was I at having a dragon's voice in my head. "W-what have I learned, besides that the world is better off with me lost in these cold forests?"

"Dear Sir Kristoff, you have learned that dragons are just as smart as you. You've learned that just because you can kill something doesn't always mean you should. And you've learned that there are consequences when you do stupid things. Now, pick yourself up off that dirty ground, and learn from your mistakes. There is hope for you yet, and there is much good you can do for this world."

I slowly stood, struggling to stay upright as my weakened body screamed at me for the abuse I'd put it through. "What good can I do, Mistress Soulreader?" I whispered, still a little shocked at the fact that I was talking to a dragon in my head.

"Kristoff, you have learned how the different dragon types live, what they eat, and more. You can use this knowledge and bring eggs of the dragon types that used to live on Taruvek back with you. You can help them repopulate Taruvek, and you can protect them from those that think like you thought, that we are no more than animals." The Soulreader paused looking deep into my eyes and

soul, and then said, *"You have the makings of a Dragon Caretaker if you let that part of yourself out. I can sense it in you..."*

"That's how I can help and do good? By becoming a Dragon Caretaker? But I know nothing about what that means." I'd never have considered such a thing, but as she looked into my soul I felt the part of me she had seen as if she had unburied it, and I realized she was right.

"I see you have realized the same thing. So will you do this, Sir Kristoff? Will you help dragons live on Taruvek once again?" she said in her gentle voice.

"I still can hardly believe this is happening to me...but, yes. Yes, I think I will. How can I find out which types belong there? And how will I know what to do as a Caretaker?" I could hardly speak the words, but the part of me she had revealed drew me in like a Leafwelder to vailo berries.

"The types that used to live on Taruvek are the Tidebringers, Leafwelders, Marshbacks, Stormrenders, and Timebenders. You must bring several eggs of each type back with you, build a sanctuary for them, and hatch and raise them." She spoke like she'd been planning this for a while.

"Alright. I shall do it. I shall return to Taruvek first and get someone building the Sanctuary while I sail back to each continent and collect the eggs. How I'll convince them to give me eggs to hatch, I do not know, but I will try," I said with a determination I barely felt.

"Good. I'm glad you will take this path, Sir Kristoff. It is the will of the gods of Light that you do this." Her voice had a note of finality to it that surprised me.

"Thank you, Soulreader, for your wisdom. I shall do the gods' will. Could you give me the direction I need to get off the island? I fear I have lost my way." I glanced around me as I spoke.

"Of course I will! But first I must heal you, so you can make it there."

"Heal me? How?" I asked, confused and exhausted.

"My magic, Kristoff, I am a Soulreader and a Healer." As she spoke I felt a strange warmth enter my chest, and spread throughout my body. It was not

painful, but it wasn't quite comfortable either as she healed me and restored my strength.

I let out a small gasp as the warmth left just as suddenly as it had started.

"Now, climb onto my back. I shall take you back myself and help you convince the Dragon Caretaker to give you eggs from the Tidebringers." As she spoke she knelt down for me to mount her.

"Thank you! May I ask what your name is?" I asked, in awe of her.

"My name is Asa. And I am happy to help you."

Secondus, 112th day of Aestas.

Asa flew me all the way to the small village of Fellinveu to speak with the Dragon Caretaker and Tidebringers.

We got into the Sanctuary quickly, since Asa was the one asking, and you don't refuse a Soulreader what it asks. As we entered the floating Sanctuary, I stopped in my tracks to gawk at it. The ceiling of the dome was fifty feet above us and was made entirely of different gems that created beautiful glittering pictures of every type of dragon on Arrovad. It was awe-inspiring to see so many precious gems in one place. Here, gemstones are as common as any other stone, and rare shells are their currency.

The Caretaker appeared then from a side room, and he was quite imposing with his great height, stark black hair, light sand-colored eyes, bright clothes, and baby dragons hanging off of every limb.

Asa continued with confidence down the hall, and I had to walk quickly to catch up.

"Try to keep your mouth closed, Sir Kristoff, or he may not take you seriously," she said with amusement in her voice.

Having a dragon talk to you in your mind is a strange thing; it's like hearing them without hearing them, and you can almost feel the brush of their mind against yours.

Anyway, I shall do my best to record our interaction with the Caretaker. Asa addressed him first, saying, *"Caretaker Bered, this Knight of Taruvek has a request to make of you, and I'll have you know I fully support him in this and I advise you do as well."*

Well, then. I'm not sure how he could possibly say no now. Asa just backed him into a corner very effectively. As I was thinking this, Asa glanced at me and her whole demeanor said, *Say something, you big dummy!*

So I said, "Caretaker Bered, my name is Sir Kristoff of Brolawskiiven Manor of the country of Ruvek on the continent of Taruvek. I come before you, a man that has been hunting dragons since early Ver. I did not know or understand the level of intelligence these creatures have, and thus I made some very big mistakes. I thankfully never got the chance to harm any of the dragons I hunted, but sadly my companions were all either killed or injured. I tell you this first so you know the truth about me. Several days ago, I lost the will to live, so weighed down was I with guilt over my actions, and then yesterday Asa came to me. She said I could still do some good in this world by bringing dragon eggs to Taruvek and creating a Dragon Sanctuary there. So Caretaker, I am here today to request enough Tidebringer eggs to begin reintroducing them to Taruvek. It will take time, and I will protect the hatchlings from others that think like I did, but returning dragons to Taruvek would help everyone." I stopped talking then, not wanting to say too much.

The Caretaker looked me up and down with a measuring eye, and said, "You are very forthright about your crimes, Sir Kristoff. What makes you think we'll trust you with something as precious as dragon eggs with a record like yours?"

"You have no reason to trust me, Caretaker. All I can say is that I am a changed man, and I truly believe this is the Lights' will for me."

"Hmm," he hummed to himself, before saying, "Let me have one day to think about it, and to speak with the dragons themselves. Were it not for Asa vouching for you, I would never consider this, and you would be in prison right now. But her advice will be taken into account."

Tertius, 113th day of Aestas.

When the Caretaker summoned us the next day, I came well-fed and well-rested for the first time in a long time. I'd also bathed and wore clothes of the Arrovadian style, which I got in the village. Of course that meant they were a little snug and long on me since I'm a bit shorter and stockier than most Arrovadians.

Once Asa and I got to the Sanctuary, I saw that there were two Tide-bringers present, both from the ocean and thus quite large. This gave me hope that maybe my request had been granted, and I glanced at Asa to see her reaction. Sure enough, she had a satisfied gleam in her soft eyes, and her tail gave a happy twitch like a cat's.

The meeting with them went well, and we will be leaving Arrovad with Tidebringer eggs from the three different sizes of Tidebringers. We will stay four more days for me to learn all I can from the Caretaker before we leave, and he is writing down everything I need to know to hatch and raise Tidebringers in a journal for me to take back with me.

I knew that this day would change my life forever. I no longer will live for killing creatures for trophies, but instead for bringing dragons back to Taruvek.

Quartus, 114th day of Aestas.

I met someone yesterday evening.

Her name is Caelan Daciana, or the Fair Wolf, as the people call her.

It was after Asa and I spent the day learning from Caretaker Bered. Asa had gone out to find food for herself, and I went to the tavern for dinner and a drink. As I sat there eating and drinking, I couldn't help but sink into depression over my dead friends. Apparently, Caelan noticed, as she came and sat at my table with her own plate of food and said, "You, Sir Taruveken, look like you need some company to get your mind off of dark things."

I could only sit there and blink at her in surprise before she grabbed my left hand and laid her palm face down on it in the Arrovadian greeting, saying as she did, "My name is Caelan Daciana, but you can call me Cael, Lany, or even Elan. Most here call me Fair Wolf, but call me by one of my nicknames. So what's your name?"

"Kristoff Brolawskiiven, but you can call me Kristoff. It's a pleasure to meet you Miss...Cael," I said, blundering my words and sounding like a dolt.

After that initial introduction we talked as if we had always been friends. Cael was one of the easiest people to talk to I'd ever met. She had such an open, friendly demeanor, her sand-colored eyes holding such pure joy and honesty, that I knew instinctively she was someone I could trust.

At one point she said, "Tell me about the other continents, Kris! What was your favorite city? What are the people there like? Ever since we found out about the other continents six years ago, I've wanted to visit them."

I smiled as I remembered the places I'd seen. "The people of Kelasinar build everything out of wood and stone. The country of Nevar specifically has built their whole society around what the dragons and their Riders can do. The Marshbacks and their Riders help farmers irrigate their fields, and the Eruptorectums help melt the snow in Ver. It's really amazing to see what they've done with the help of so many dragons and Riders. On Dalnar, they have a palace and city made entirely of Sanddigger's glass, and the jungles there have more birds than you've ever seen and more bugs, and the people there use gems as their currency."

She could hardly believe all I told her about the food, cultures, and places I'd seen.

Even when it came out that I'd been hunting the dragons, she showed shock and horror for a moment, before her face transformed into one of understanding and sorrow for what I'd lost due to my mistakes.

She told me very bluntly that had she met me while I was still hunting them, she likely would have beaten me to a pulp. And somehow I didn't doubt she would have tried, and based on the diamond blade axes she had on her back, and the way she moved with confidence and surety, she may have given me a run for my money.

As we talked long into the night, I wished my time with her wouldn't end, but that we might continue to be friends even after I left this cold but beautiful place.

Primus, 116th day of Aestas.

I've spent the last two days with Caretaker Bered, and then the evening exploring Fellinveu with Cael. It was a lovely time altogether. I wish I didn't have to leave.

Today at midday Cael, Caretaker Bered, and I all went to the temple together, to pray and worship. I must say the Arrovadian temple is every bit as beautiful as the Dalnarian one. It has a larger central dome with seven smaller ones floating on the water around it. The center dome is built out of diamond, and each of the ones around it are built out of a different type of gem. The sunlight is refracted into millions of rainbows in the central dome by the diamonds.

I believe I've learned more here on Arrovad, and the other continents I've traveled, than I have my entire life back on Taruvek. I was so wrong about dragons, and my mistakes have cost me dearly. But I am ready to move on to this next chapter of my life, as a Dragon Caretaker.

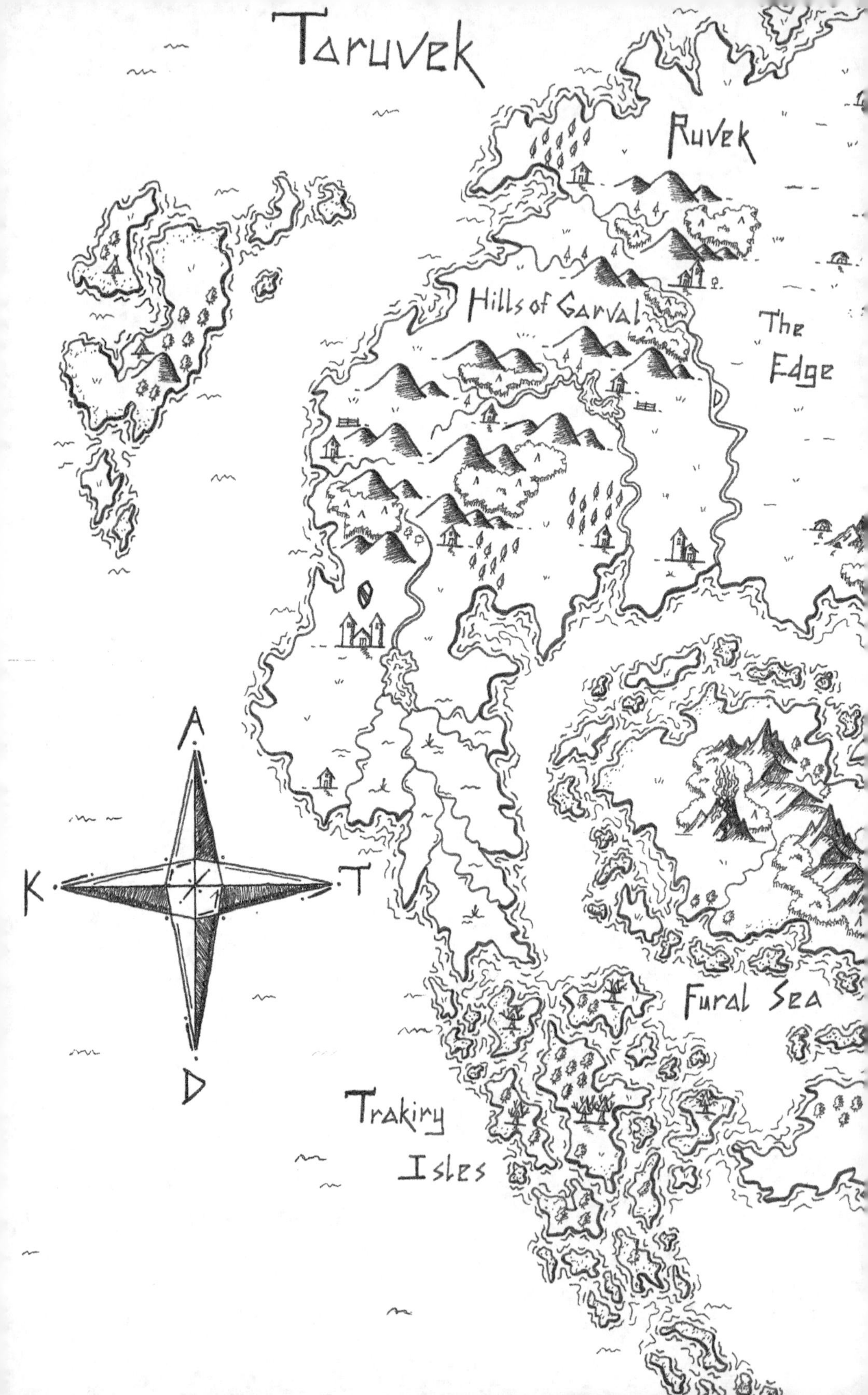

Taruvek
Ruvek
Hills of Garval
The Edge
A
K
T
D
Fural Sea
Trakiry
Isles

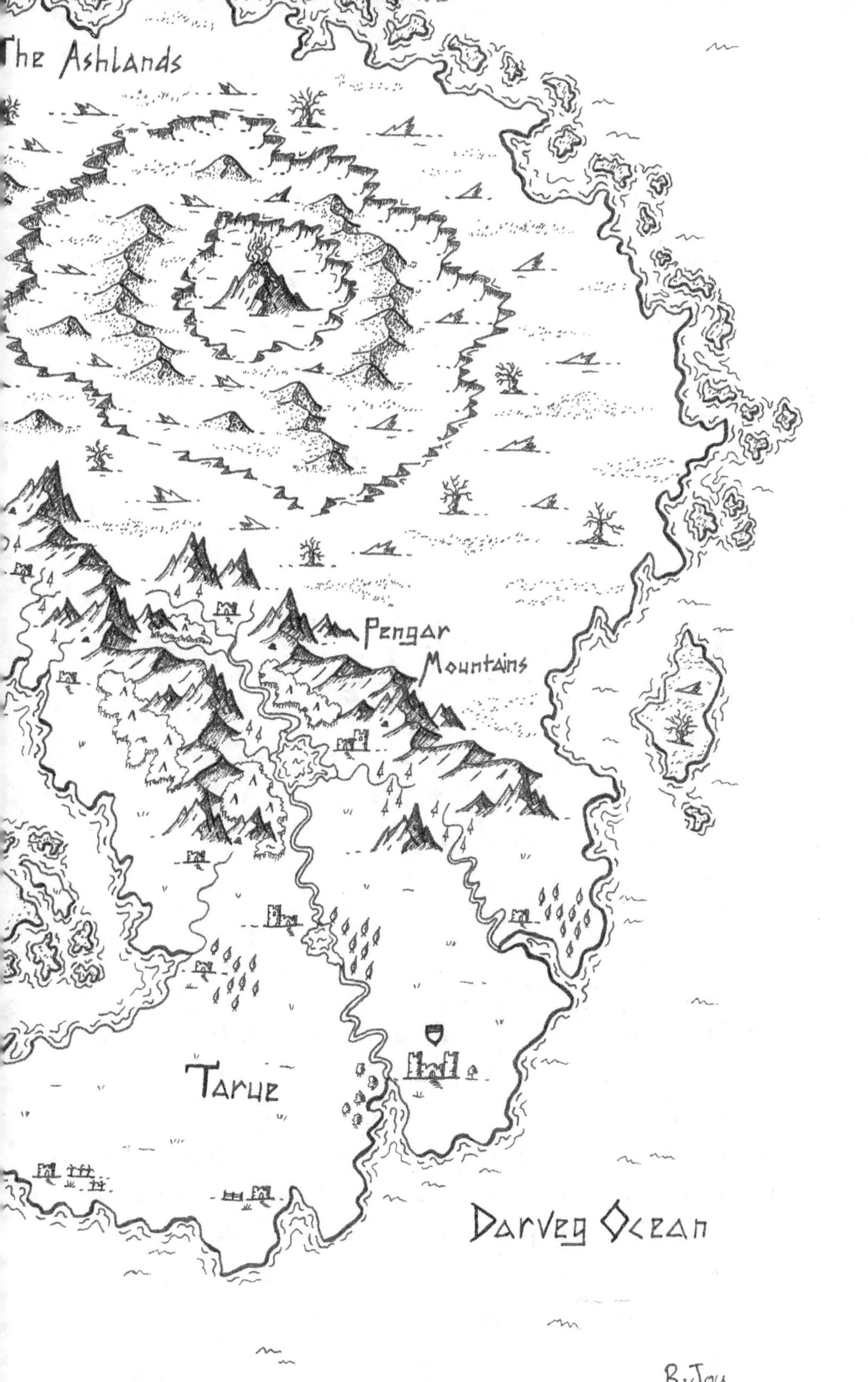

The Ashlands
Pengar Mountains
Tarue
Darveg Ocean
R. Joy
2/25/21

TARUVEK

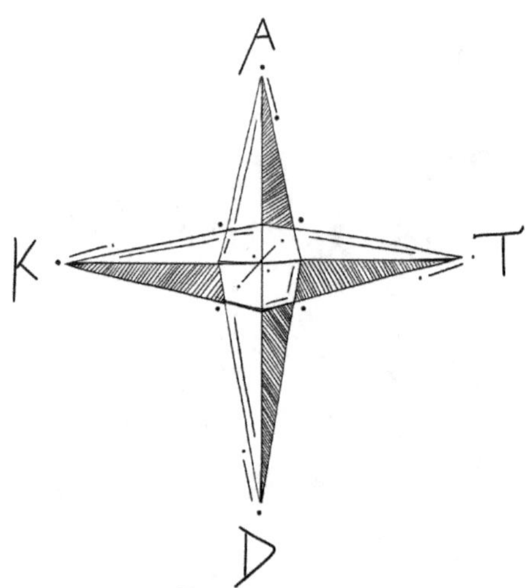

Secondus, 117th day of Aestas.

Early this morning, I said goodbye to Caretaker Bered and Cael. She gave me a big hug and whispered into my ear, "When your Sanctuary is built, I will come visit you!"

To which I said, "Please do! I'd love to show you around Taruvek!" Then, turning to Asa, I said, "Asa, you have changed my life, and I can never repay you. Thank you for your help, and may the Lights bless you!"

Asa's eyes sparkled at me in amusement as she said, *"Kristoff, do you really think I am about to let you go on your own?"*

"What do you mean?" I asked, hoping she meant what I thought she did but needing to be sure.

She looked into me again, like the first time we met. *"I knew the moment I felt you enter that forest that you were the right person for this mission and that I must help you somehow. At first I didn't know how or why the gods would wish me to help such an arrogant trophy hunter as yourself, but then I felt the weight of your guilt and grief, and I knew what they wanted me to do. So yes, I will go with you, and I will help you bring dragons back to Taruvek."*

So now here we are on an Arrovadian ship pulled by four massive elephant seals bound for Taruvek with our precious cargo, the Tidebringer eggs, stowed carefully away. I am anxious to get home, and make my request to the rulers of Ruvek, Tarue, and the Tribal Heads of the Edgelands for the building of the Dragon Sanctuary at the bottom of the Edge where Ruvek and Tarue meet. Hopefully they'll grant me my request.

Secondus, 7th day of Cado.

It's officially Cado now, my birth month. We have just reached Taruvek and unloaded everything.

I won't rest easy until I have put these eggs in the safe keeping of someone I can trust, but everyone I trusted before thinks the same way I used to about dragons.

Maybe I can entrust them to the tribes of the Edgelands. After all, they believed in the existence and intelligence of dragons far before even the Shadow Wars brought their existence to light on Taruvek.

Quartus, 14th day of Cado.

I've been in meetings with the rulers and nobles of Tarue and Ruvek for two days straight already, and they still haven't accepted my reasons for building the Sanctuary in the Edgelands instead of the capital of either country. They refuse to accept the fact that it can't be ruled by either country even though I've explained that's how it is on every other continent. And of course, once I convinced one ruler, their nobles became upset and started arguing again. Somehow it wasn't hard to convince them that introducing dragons back to Taruvek was a good idea, as it means more power for each nation once there are Dragon Riders.

I'm not sure how long it will take me to convince them that this is the right way, but Asa and I will not relent.

Secondus, 17th day of Cado.

We have finally convinced the rulers of Ruvek and Tarue that the place we've chosen for the Sanctuary is the best option. It took us a full week to do so, but it's done now.

Honestly I think it was Asa more than anything that convinced them; after all, when you feel the annoyance of a Soulreader dragon pressing in on your mind, you do whatever it takes to appease her as quickly as possible...

So we are now back on the road, heading to the Edgelands.

Quartus, 19th day of Cado.

With the help of the tribes of the Edge, I found a good building site. It's by the Fural Sea, so the Tidebringers will have a place to swim and hunt, but also near to the plains of the Edgelands, the Pengar Mountains, and the few forests we have there. I hope with the return of Leafwelders we will see the forests here on Taruvek increase as well.

Back in Ver, when I first sailed to Kelasinar with my friends and began my quest, I had no idea I'd be coming back with dragon eggs instead of heads. I just hope I can protect them from those that might wish to harm them.

Secondus, 22nd day of Cado.

Things are going surprisingly quickly with the Sanctuary. I've found a builder and drawn up the plans.

Then I found people to start a garden to feed everyone working here, and others to start our own fuel refinery since we're so far away from any of the others. I even found someone to leave the eggs with. Her name is Benta, and she is distantly related to the famous hunter Yaegar Haddan, who became a Legend of the Shadow Wars.

I feel comfortable leaving now that things are in place here and the eggs are safe. We shall sail to Dalnar first for Leafwelder and Stormrender eggs. Then to Kelasinar for the Marshback, Eruptorectum, and Timebender eggs.

Secondus, 42nd day of Cado.

We've just landed on Dalnar, and the journey here went smoothly for once. The last few weeks have been very busy, even though I've been sailing. I've been training with Asa a lot to hone my growing abilities, and I've been coming up with how I can convince these next two Caretakers to give us eggs. Especially since Caretaker Ilaria actually tried to find and stop us when we were here last. On top of that, I've been working out more of the details for the Sanctuary back on Taruvek.

Quartus, 44th day of Cado.

I ran into some trouble at an inn we stayed at as we were traveling.

Asa had gone out to find food, and I was eating supper. Well, it seems word of me and my previous quest has spread, because I was grabbed at the inn by a group of men and brought to the Enforcers for questioning. I did not fight them at all or even try to explain my change of heart to them, for I knew in their state of anger they would not believe me without Asa there. So I went with them to the Enforcers and hoped Asa would come soon. I tried to explain the situation to the Enforcers, but they heard the words "Dragon Hunter" and threw me into a hanging cage high above the forest floor. There were two other prisoners in separate cages; one was passed out and looked to be drunk, and the other glowered at me and looked like a thief.

I sat there in the cage just waiting for Asa. I had no doubt she'd find me and give these Enforcers an earful, but I didn't know when that would be, so I made myself as comfortable as possible and closed my eyes to rest.

I woke up suddenly, not knowing when I had fallen asleep. There was a commotion in the building where the Enforcers were, and I could distinctly hear Asa's voice projecting loudly to all that were in the area as she said, *"Did you even listen to him?! How dare you just put him in a cage like a common criminal! You should be ashamed of yourselves. You don't deserve to be called Enforcers if you aren't going to actually enforce true justice. This man has suffered his punishment for his deeds by the Lights' hands. You have no right to touch him now. He is on a mission for the gods of Light, and you just delayed him. Open this door. Now! Get him out of the cage!"*

As she said the last bit, the door to the deck from which they reeled in the cages opened and out came two wide-eyed Enforcers behind Asa. One started cranking the lever which swung my cage towards the deck, and Asa said, *"Kristoff, did they harm you in any way? I will be talking to the Caretaker, and they will be punished accordingly."*

She fumed as they opened my cage and unbound my wrists and ankles, but once I was free I laid my hand on her face and looked into her wise, gentle eyes, which were lit from within with a righteous anger, and said, "Asa. They did nothing wrong. If I were in their position I would have done the same thing. I was a Dragon Hunter, and though as you've said I have been punished, they could not have known that. Don't have them punished on my account."

Asa's eyes narrowed at me as she struggled to let go of her anger, but then they softened as she saw into my soul, and she said, *"You gentlemen should be thankful he is so understanding. I will let this go, but you will do better in the future."*

The older of the two Enforcers bowed slightly to Asa and said, "Thank you, Wise One! We are truly regretful of our mistreatment of Sir Kristoff." Then turning to me, he placed a hand over his heart while bowing shallowly and said, "Sir Kristoff, please accept our most humble apology. We had no idea who you now are."

I knew they only apologized because of their fear of Asa, but I nodded and gave a slight bow back as I said, "Your apology is accepted. I understand completely why you did what you did. And I commend your protection of the dragons."

Asa and I took our leave after that and continued on our journey since it was dawn by that time.

Tertius, 53rd day of Cado.

We are just leaving the Dalnarian Dragon Sanctuary, and I must record the events of the past week and a half while it's still fresh in my mind, for I was too busy to record it as it happened.

Caretaker Ilaria's Sanctuary is located in a remote village called Visim in the territory of Razidaln. This small village is built in the treetops, unlike other towns we've visited here that are built lower in the trees. It's like entering another world as monkeys, birds, and other jungle animals go from branch to branch right at your eye level or just above your head. The people here have tiny little monkeys, colorful birds, and tree cats as pets.

Asa and I made our way through the village towards a ring of very old trees, which are connected with covered walkways that stretch from room to room of the Dragon Sanctuary.

We received many strange looks along the way because we make quite the odd pair since I'm clearly from Taruvek, where there are no dragons, and she is clearly from Arrovad, where Soulreaders are lighter than the ones on Dalnar.

As we entered the main room of the Sanctuary, I couldn't help but look around as everything was decorated with beautiful feathers, shells, and colorful glass beads. The room was large and circular, with round windows that were open to the forest breeze outside, and through them the songs of the jungle birds serenaded us.

After studying the room, I turned my gaze to Caretaker Ilaria, and I was surprised to see she was much younger than I would have expected; in fact she was not much older than me. She was short and strong in stature, and I had no doubt she could take on any knight to protect her dragon charges. Her skin is a darker, richer mahogany brown than most Dalnarians I've seen, her bright red hair is long and wavy, and her eyes are a striking blue.

As we reached her, I said, "Caretaker Ilaria, I am Sir Kristoff of Brolawski-iven Manor in Ruvek, and this is Asa, a Soulreader from Arrovad. I am here today to petition you for assistance in starting to reintroduce dragons back onto Taruvek. We were given six Tidebringer eggs from Arrovad to hatch and raise in our Sanctuary that is being built as we speak, but we need other types as well. One type is the Leafwelder, another is the Stormrender. Would you be willing to ask the dragons for these eggs for me to bring to Taruvek?"

"Before you respond, Caretaker Ilaria, I wish you to know that I have been called by the gods of Light to help Sir Kristoff on this mission. Dragons must return to Taruvek, but we need your help for that to happen." Asa spoke to both of us at the same time, and I could see the Caretaker's surprise at the fervor in her words.

She'd successfully done it again. I would never get used to how she could back such powerful people into a corner that they could not get out of just by how she worded things. She clearly understands her power as a Soulreader and is willing to use it.

"Well, you don't beat around the bush at all, do you. But tell me, are you the same knight I was searching for that was here leading a group of men hunting for dragons in Aestas?" she asked, gazing at me with a look in her vibrant eyes that told me she already knew the answer.

I bowed my head, ashamed and guilty, as I said, "Yes, Caretaker, I am sad to say I am that same knight. I have no excuses for my actions back in Ver and Aestas. All I can say is that on Arrovad, I realized how wrong I was about dragons and how big the mistakes I made were. I will never stop regretting and feeling guilty for what I did, and for the men that died because of my actions. But now I am doing my best to do good for this world, and the dragons, by bringing them back to Taruvek and becoming the first Dragon Caretaker Taruvek has had in centuries."

"I'm glad you're honest about your mistakes. How can we be sure you're a changed man, though? Asa speaking for you definitely helps, but I want to know why you think I or the dragons should trust you?" She spoke in a tone that was hard to decipher.

I could see the interest in her eyes as she studied me, but I could also see she had made up her mind already, though I didn't know if it was for or against me yet.

"I can't honestly tell you anything about me or my history that would make you trust me, but I can say this. As I lay under the trees of Arrovad, giving up on life, the gods of Light gave me a second chance in this world. They sent Asa to me to give me guidance in order for me to finally do something good for this world. So don't trust me or my word because I am not worthy of it, but if you trust the gods of Light then you can trust that they are now guiding me, and my quest is their quest. I swear this to you, on my honor as a knight of Ruvek."

"Hmm, well I will have to call a meeting with the leaders of those dragons before we can make our decision, and I'm certain they will wish to meet you and speak with Asa before agreeing to anything. How long will you be staying here?" she asked.

"We will stay as long as is needed, Caretaker. And we'd be happy to meet with them. If they agree to my request, I'd like to stay here for a short time to learn all I can about these types of dragons and how to hatch and raise them."

The Caretaker smiled slightly at me, nodding as she said, "That is very wise of you, Sir Kristoff."

"Thank you, Caretaker Ilaria. I appreciate your willingness to hear me out." I bowed low to her.

"Well, I shall call a meeting for tomorrow at the earliest time we can. For now you are welcome to use the quarters you've been given, and you may tour the Dragon Sanctuary while you stay as well to start learning," the Caretaker said.

"I like this one, Kristoff. She can teach you much that the other Caretaker couldn't." Asa spoke to us both as she looked at Ilaria.

Ilaria smiled and touched a hand to Asa's forehead as she said, "Thank you, Wise One. I am glad Kristoff has you to keep him in line."

After our meeting with Caretaker Ilaria, we met with the Leafwelders and Stormrenders, and let me tell you, as wise and gentle as Asa's voice is, the Leafwelder Elowen's voice was quiet like a breeze whispering through dry leaves in Cado, and the Stormrender Jorah's voice was like the gentle sound of rain falling through leaves. They asked me some questions, but I think it was the knowledge that I was truly a Dragon Caretaker now more than anything I said that convinced them to give me the eggs.

We stayed five more days to learn from Caretaker Ilaria and the dragons themselves. I also had her write everything we needed to know about these dragons in my Caretaker journal. She agreed to come to Taruvek a year from now to check over everything.

Our time at the sanctuary was well spent, as I learned so much from Ilaria. She has such a deep connection to the dragons, and understands them on a level I haven't seen before.

One day while we were there, Caretaker Ilaria asked if I'd like to fly with the dragons and her to see the dragonets take their first flights, and of course

I said yes. What an amazing opportunity to see a dragon take its first flight. I felt privileged to be invited.

We took off with me riding Asa and Caretaker Ilaria riding Jorah. Where we were headed, I did not know, but the flight through the trees was amazing.

Suddenly, as we broke free of the trees, the sky around us filled with dragons of every type found on Dalnar and of all ages. The dragonets were riding on the older dragons' backs. Immediately my mind was overwhelmed by their thoughts and excitement. It happened so unexpectedly, like a wall in my mind had been knocked down, and now everything that had been held back by it was released like a flood. I nearly lost my hold on Asa when it happened, but then her mind enveloped mine like a warm blanket, dampening the sound of their thoughts. *"Hold on, Kristoff. Focus on blocking them out yourself, and Caretaker Ilaria and I will teach you how to let just one in at a time later when we're safely on the ground."* She spoke gently but firmly to me.

"Thank you, Asa," was all I could manage through the mind link, as my focus was on silencing the cacophony of dragon voices.

She seemed startled but pleased. *"Very good, Kristoff. It often takes Caretakers months to learn to mind speak. But focus on blocking for now instead."*

When we were above a long grassy valley, the dragons carrying the young ones flew just a bit lower, and then the first brave dragonet leapt forth, spreading its wings to catch the wind. After a moment more started to follow suit. They were a bit shaky at first, wobbling on the air currents like a child first learning to walk, but as they glided towards the ground, flapping their wings to slow down, they gained confidence, and a few circled back around instead of landing. One landed a bit roughly, tumbling through the grass and coming to a very ungraceful stop in a pile of limbs and wings. There were a few more mishaps as they flew, such as one crashing into another one, but none of them got hurt.

After we returned, Ilaria led the dragons and dragonets back to their separate wings of the Sanctuary.

My head ached from the amount of dragon minds I could feel in the vicinity. Asa was helping blanket me from them, but their constant chatter in the background of my mind still wore on me.

"Your abilities are growing more by the day, Kristoff. Soon enough you'll be able to block out the mental noise yourself," she said in a gentle tone.

"Thank you, Asa. I appreciate your help, I hope that ability comes sooner rather than later. You've been nothing but good to me on this journey. Would you consider staying on Taruvek and helping me with the dragonets after we've gathered all the eggs?"

"Of course I'll be staying with you, Kristoff! Do you think I'm helping you with all of this just to leave you? No, I'm afraid you're stuck with me. Of course I'll need to return to Arrovad every seven cycles to breed and lay my eggs, but I won't be gone for more than a cycle each time."

I nodded, smiling at her as I said, *"Thank you, Asa, I am very lucky to call you my friend!"*

She just laughed and went back to eating her meal of nuts and berries.

Amazingly, Elowen has decided to accompany me first to Kelasinar and then to Taruvek to help me raise the dragonets when they hatch. One of the eggs we are taking is from her and her mate who died of natural causes soon after they last bred.

Quintus, 65th day of Cado.

We're just over half way to Kelasinar now, plus it's my birth month celebration day! I've been studying what both the Caretakers have written down for me, and it's taught me so much. Asa has been teaching me about the history of dragons as well. Seems she is much older than I first realized.

Tertius, 73rd day of Cado.

We've reached Kelasinar! Caretaker Delbert's Sanctuary is just a few days' ride away on horseback, but on dragon it is much shorter. I hope we can convince him to give us the eggs. From what I've heard, not many people know him very well.

Quintus, 75th day of Cado.

He gave us the eggs!

After hearing about how Asa helped me, and the other Caretakers giving me eggs, Caretaker Delbert and the dragons willingly gave me a few of each type. He is a quiet, reclusive man, and thus he didn't especially want me staying there long. So as soon as I knew what I needed to and he'd written down instructions, we took our leave, and we are now sailing home to Taruvek, for our quest for the eggs is complete and now begins the preparation for them to be hatched.

Dragon eggs won't hatch until the right conditions for them are met, such as extreme heat for the Eruptorectum eggs, and lots of humidity and hot mud baths for the Marshback eggs.

Dragon eggs are hatchable even after decades when stored right, thankfully, though it won't take decades for the Sanctuary to be built.

Quintus, 90th day of Cado.

We've reached Taruvek, and now we are traveling to the build site for the First Dragon Sanctuary of Taruvek.

I am anxious to see what progress has been made on it since we left. Asa and Elowen are not strong enough to carry me and all the eggs we now have, so we have hired an elk team to pull a wagon with the eggs. It will take us four days to get there, so we will need to stop at inns along the way. Hopefully they will let Asa and Elowen stay in their own rooms.

Secondus, 92nd day of Cado.

I don't know why I worried about the inns. If Asa can convince rulers and Caretakers to give us what we need, an innkeeper is a piece of cake for her. She even convinced them to give her and Elowen food they could eat since they eat more plants, nuts, and berries.

We should arrive at the Sanctuary in two days.

Quartus, 99th day of Cado.

We're at the building site in the Edgelands now!

The Sanctuary is coming along nicely. Hopefully it will be finished by Ver, as that is when the first eggs will hatch.

It will be built out of several different metals, including some of the rare, extremely strong lunametallum, and it will have a wing off the main hall for each type of dragon. It will look like a giant, six-spoked wheel when we're finished, with the round dome center hall and the wings branching off from there all the way around it.

For now we are living in tents like the tribes live in. I was surprised at how okay Asa and Elowen were when they saw the large dragon rib cages the tribes use for shelter and for carrying their supplies. I suppose since those dragons died in the Lunar Disintegration and the Days of Darkness, not by the tribes themselves, it's alright to use their bones. But still, it is strange to sleep within the ribcage of a huge dragon.

The tribesmen are in awe of Asa and Elowen, and they treat them, and by extension me, with utmost respect. I suppose it shouldn't be surprising after the role they played in the Shadow Wars, fighting alongside dragons. And before that even, they communicated with the spirits of the dead wild dragons that used to live all over Taruvek.

Secondus, 52nd day of Hiems.

Caelan arrived today!

She sent a message on the ship that left a week before hers, which thankfully gave me enough time to prepare a place for her to stay.

She ran and threw herself into my arms in her usual way, and I just held her for a moment, afraid to let go. I worried that it had been too long since we first met, or that I may have changed too much.

When she let go of me, she gripped my hands and said, "I've waited so long to sail the ocean, and I finally had a good reason to do it! How have you been, Kris? I see the Sanctuary is coming along very nicely."

I chuckled to myself at her exuberance as I said, "I'm so glad I could give you a reason to see another part of the world. I'm doing well, with Asa's help I was able to get all the eggs, and now we are racing the clock until the first of them hatch."

"Oh, how exciting! I can't wait to see them hatch. Baby dragons are the cutest things ever. You know what? I am quite famished. My only complaint about the voyage is the food. I got so sick of pickled or salted fish and dry bread. I want to try all the foods you have here on Taruvek."

She chatted with everyone she met as she walked around the camp and introduced herself to each worker.

I just sat back and watched as she made friends with everyone, as is her way.

Caelan is a woman who loves freely and sees the good in those around her even when it's shadowed by the bad, and she makes you want to come out of those shadows and step into the light.

Quintus, 60th day of Hiems.

The main hall of the Sanctuary is finished now, as are the living quarters for us humans! The Timebender and Leafwelder wings are next, as those are the first eggs that will hatch in Ver. We will finish the other wings in the order the eggs will hatch. It is so beautiful already. The center dome is made of the silvery-blue lunametallum, which shimmers as if it is rippling even though it isn't, and the wings off of it will each be made of a different metal. The windows in the dome, and in the walls, are made from many different colors of sea glass, creating rainbows of light. We have even begun to build a small temple to the gods of Light separate from the Sanctuary for those that live here to worship in. I am so thankful for the help of the tribes and Caelan in building this Dragon Sanctuary. Without them, none of this would be possible.

Tertius, 83rd day of Hiems.

An Ember tree appeared during the night!

What a shock it was when I walked out into the brisk morning light only to come face to bark with a large gnarled trunk. For a moment I stood there dumbstruck with no idea what I was looking at, but then it moved a branch in a waving type motion.

I slowly waved a hand back, and said, "Hello, there…"

The tree seemed pleased with my greeting and moved backwards a bit to let me pass. As I edged around it I studied it. It had a very thick gnarled trunk, and wasn't more than a single story high. Its roots crawled out over the ground like tentacles as it moved, and here and there I could see glowing silvery-gold sap running down it. The bark was a deep orange-red color, and I could just see some red buds beginning to form at the tips of its branches.

Throughout the rest of the day it followed me as I worked around the Sanctuary. I gave it some food scraps from our noon meal, which it consumed quite quickly. Seems like it's going to stick around, for now at least.

Ember trees are extremely rare, and from them came the Legend of the Phoenix. They came to be when a few of the Legends of the Shadow Wars defended themselves against an Ash tree that was attacking them and trying to eat them alive. When the Legends used their lightning and lava magic against the tree, it lit on fire and burned for a full day and night, but it did not die. Their magic killed the curse of death that had plagued the tree for centuries, and from the ash and flame a new tree was formed, they called it the Ember tree. This tree fought beside the Legends in the final battle against the Shadows, and the stories Tom used to tell us say it was killed, but from the flames of its internal everburning fire a seed took shape and began to grow. So it lived on, and as it reached its maturity once again, a beautiful red bird called the Phoenix came to nest in its strong branches. This bird helped keep the pests away from the young tree, so in return the tree guarded the bird, and its young, from predators. Thus the Legend of the Phoenix was born, for when the tree once again burst into flames the Phoenix took flight, and the people who saw it thought it was the Phoenix not the Ember tree being reborn...

Primus, 11th day of Ver.

The first eggs have hatched at last!

They are baby Timebenders, and they are magnificent. There are two pairs of them, each from different parents. One male is garnet in color with tiny pearl colored spikes, the other is ruby with pearl spikes. One girl is amethyst with opal spikes, and the other is alexandrite with opal spikes. I can't wait for the rest of the eggs to hatch!

They thankfully cannot use their magic yet, otherwise we'd be in for a world of difficulty trying to keep track of baby dragons that can speed up and slow down time. They follow me everywhere, and without Asa, Elowen, and the Caretaker journal I'd have no idea what I was doing, but we're getting by alright. Caelan has also been a huge help in getting everything ready. She's decided to stay here on Taruvek for the foreseeable future, which I'm very happy about.

The bond I have with each of the dragons here grows daily. Their minds and thoughts are easy to reach now, as if they are tied to my own by cords of light.

With my Caretaker abilities growing I can feel my touch and strength have been enhanced by Elowen's Leafwelder magic, my balance and perception by Asa's Spirit magic, and now my hearing and stealth by the baby Timebenders' magic. Soon enough when the other dragonets hatch I'll gain other enhancements as well, such as sight and speed from the Stormrender's magic, taste and endurance by the Tidebringer's magic, and smell and agility by the Eruptorectum magic.

Being a Caretaker of dragons may not give me magic like being a Rider would, but it gives me all the physical and sensory enhancements they gain from being mind linked to a dragon, and I must say they are very handy when tending to mischievous little dragons.

Secondus, 22nd day of Ver.

The dragonets are growing quickly, and we have started incubating the Leafwelder eggs, so they will hatch before the month is over. Elowen will help me raise them, and thank goodness for that as Leafwelders are the most mischievous of all the breeds.

It is amazing just how much the Timebender babies can eat, and the amount of energy they have. I've had to hire another farmer to raise more animals for meat just for the dragonets.

Tertius, the 33rd day of Ver, 2,634ALD.

It is the one cycle anniversary of the beginning of our quest today.

My heart is heavy remembering the friends I lost on that gods forsaken quest I came up with.

I have recently visited all the families of the ones that died, and some were more welcoming than others, understandably. I put up a plaque in honor of each one at the Dragon Sanctuary to remember them and the lessons I learned.

I also visited those that survived and found that they have moved on as much as they can from what happened. John has taken up working at a Shard Ring making facility where he can work sitting down due to his leg. Tobias is living with one of his siblings and their family; because of his head injury he can no longer live alone, and unfortunately it is unlikely that he will ever marry. Ed has taken up building because he can use his metal hand like a hammer. Rick is still terrified of squirrels, but since he lives in the middle of a city working as Rule Keeper, he rarely sees any. They were all shocked to hear about my new mission, but when they met Asa they understood.

Afterword

Thank you so much for reading my novella, I truly hope you enjoyed it!

If you would like to get exclusive sneak peaks at my future books, participate in some fantasy fun with me, and help me with future books, then you can join my Monthly Fantasy Periodical which you can sign up for through my website https://rjoyfantasy.wixsite.com/my-site-1 where you'll receive a free short story! You can also follow me on Tiktok - @fantasy_writer_r.joy Instagram - @fantasy_writer_r.joy, and Facebook - Fantasy Writer R.Joy

Also, as an indie author reviews are how our books climb the ranks on Amazon, but they also help us know what our readers enjoyed about our stories so we can do more of that. So please consider leaving an honest review so other readers can find and enjoy my story too.

ALSO BY

If you're interested in more books by me, you can check out my fantasy short story Hunt for the Dragon Egg Thief which takes place just before this book. Here's a short blurb for it:

The most respected dragon alive. A young warrioress. And a thief trying to bring creatures of darkness back from the Void.

When Frostcreeper dragon eggs begin to go missing, Soulreader dragon Asa and the human Caelan Daciana are assigned to hunt them down.

They must rescue them before they hatch or worse, are destroyed. If they don't, Asa's worst fears may come to pass, and many lives will be lost.

Will Asa and Caelan find the stolen dragon eggs before it's too late? Or will the past repeat itself?

Get your copy on Amazon for 99 cents, or for Free through my Monthly Fantasy Periodical which you can sign up for on my website https://rjoyfantasy.wixsite.com/my-site-1

ACKNOWLEDGMENTS

First off I must thank my family for their support and encouragement as I chased the dream of being a fantasy author. You guys are the best!

Special thanks to my mother for home educating me, always telling me to write my stories down, and being one of my biggest fans from the very beginning.

Also, to my niece Caralynn for always wanting to hear my stories, and for being my other biggest fan.

I must also thank my fellow fantasy author and good friend J.D.Z, author of the Zero Chronicles, for always being willing to bounce ideas around with me, and for being the accountability and writing partner I needed.

Special thanks also goes to my Seven Sisters critique group for helping me make my books the best they can be. Author H.M Brandon, Bv Sloan, Aimee Clinton, Moa Erikson, Heather Ashbury, and Chelsey Fay, you ladies are amazing!

To all my beta readers, thank you for your honest feedback. It helped me grow as a writer.

To my editor Belinda, thank you for kindly pointing out my many mistakes, but also some of my strengths. I couldn't have done this without you.

Thank you to my cover designer Ethrics Dream Designs & Art for the awesome cover.

Finally thank you to all who buy and read this book, and especially those who take the time to review it!

ABOUT AUTHOR

R.Joy is a small produce farmer by day, and a fantasy writer and artist by night. From a young age she created worlds and stories in her mind, and developed a deep love for reading and watching fantasy. Her favorite books are The Inheritance Cycle by Christopher Paolini, The Advent Mage Cycle by Honor Raconteur, and the Lord of the Rings by J.R .R. Tolkien. When she isn't farming or writing R. Joy can often be found playing games with her family or spending time with her many chickens, her pet goose named Clover, her 2 Golden Retrievers (Prince and Gloria), and her cat named Cloud Dancing.